Whispers in Autumn

M. Jean Pike

Black Lyon Publishing, LLC

WHISPERS IN AUTUMN
Copyright © 2010 by M. JEAN PIKE

Our books may be ordered through your local bookstore or by visiting the publisher:

www.BlackLyonPublishing.com

Black Lyon Publishing, LLC
PO Box 567
Baker City, OR 97814

This is a work of fiction. All of the characters, names, events, organizations and conversations in this novel are either the products of the author's vivid imagination or are used in a fictitious way for the purposes of this story.

ISBN-10:   1-934912-24-7
ISBN-13:   978-1-934912-24-9
Library of Congress Control Number: 2010920802

Written, published and printed in
the United States of America.

Black Lyon Paranormal Romance

For my dad, who has never believed in ghosts,
but always believed in me.

Chapter One

The murder investigation had exhausted her, both emotionally and physically.

Standing in front of the mirror at the Hope Haven Gas Mart, Dove shed her jeans and sneakers and pulled on panty hose, dress and pumps. She rummaged in her bag for a tube of lipstick, the only makeup she owned, and applied a splash of color to her lips. It was too little, too late, she thought. The shimmering copper only served to accentuate the ghostly pallor of her skin and dark shadows beneath her eyes. She'd planned to go with Emma to the salon this morning and have the stylist apply whatever miracle cosmetics would conceal this evidence of eight weeks of brutal days and sleepless nights. Now there wasn't time to do more than gloss her lips and run a brush through her long, dark hair. She was already late and she still had to fill the tank.

She'd set out late last night, slinking away in the dark like a criminal to avoid being followed. She should have arrived hours ago, but early morning construction on the highway had slowed her progress to a crawl, turning a seven-hour drive into nearly ten. Then she'd missed the turn to the campground—twice. She dug her cell phone out of her purse, thinking to call for directions, only to discover she'd let the battery die. It wasn't like Dove Denning to be frazzled. In forty years she'd seen more of life than most people twice her age and she'd learned a long time before not to sweat the small stuff. But it also wasn't like her to show up late for important occasions like a dear friend's wedding. By now Emma must be frantic thinking she wasn't going to show.

The tears of frustration that came all too easily anymore filled her eyes and she fought against the strangling fear that she was spinning out of control. All her life she'd relied only on herself, but since the investigation she found herself second-guessing her instincts, constantly looking over her shoulder. And she was coming unglued.

It's over, Dove, she reminded herself. It's time to move on. She wouldn't allow herself to come unraveled thinking about the investigation, the trial, or the threats of a faceless stranger. Not here and not now, not on Emma's wedding day.

With this thought firmly in mind, she grabbed up her dirty clothes and stuffed them in her bag. With one last glance in the wavy mirror, she slung her bag over her shoulder and hurried through the gas mart, pausing long enough to fill a cup with Colombian Dark Roast on her way out the door.

By now the impossibly long line of cars at the pump had dwindled to two. She drove past the first pump, where a man filled a shiny, red Escalade. She backed her Impala up to the pump ahead of him and dug out her credit card. Stepping out of the car, she slid it into the appropriate slot and waited for authorization.

"Come on, already." She tapped her foot, her impatience flaring.

"Ma'am?"

She turned sharply, her eyes moving over the man behind her in swift appraisal. He was approximately forty-five years old, with a quality of roughness that said the years had been hard lived. At five-foot seven or eight he was only slightly taller than she stood in her heels, but he looked sturdy, like a man accustomed to hard physical labor. His dark blond hair teetered on the edge of brown, and his eyes, definitely his best feature, were a pale shade of blue. He looked harmless enough, standing there in the golden October sunshine. Still …

"Why don't you let me do that for you?" he said, surprising her further.

"Excuse me?"

"Your gas. Let me pump it for you. I'd hate to see you spill on that pretty dress."

She glanced down at the sheer, cream-colored gown that fell to her ankles. With its intricate bead work and embroidered hem it was too formal for a country wedding, let alone pumping gas. Still, she glanced into the stranger's eyes, wondering why he would possibly care. Under her scrutiny, his face colored with embarrassment and Dove's suspicions began to ease. Small town manners, she thought, all at once remembering her own.

"I'd appreciate that."

"How much are you getting?"

"Fill it," she said, climbing back behind the wheel.

She watched in the rearview mirror as he removed the gas cap and slid the nozzle inside. His sleeve rode up and she caught a glimpse of a tattoo on his biceps, a bird of some sort sitting on a branch, the entire piece underscored with a flourish of intricate cursive script. Obviously a woman's name. A current interest, she wondered idly, or some long-forgotten lover? Her glance traveled back to his face, interesting in its contours and contradictions. Weathered, she thought, while at the same time, strangely youthful. His lips were on the fleshy side, curving upward at the corners in a hint of a smile that Dove found immensely appealing. A familiar prickling sensation began in her hands, telling her she'd gazed too long, too hard, into his face.

"Oh, please," she whispered. "Not now."

Regardless, the prickling raced through her veins and became a thousand pinpoints of light and heat exploding inside her until she was completely absorbed by them. An image of the man lying prostrate on the sand filled her mind, his anguished cry hurling upward toward a silent moon. Feeling his pain, she was gripped by a sorrow so profound it stole her breath away. She clamped her eyes shut and fought to drive the image from her mind. When she opened them again the man was standing at her window, regarding her thoughtfully.

"Are you all right?"

"Yes, I …" A tremor rippled through her as the image faded away. "I'm just trying to get my bearings." Her gaze returned to his face. "Thank you for pumping my gas."

"Pleasure's mine."

His eyes lingered on hers and she pulled in a breath. Regaining her composure, she said, "I'm trying to find a place called Shadow Lake Campground. I'm supposed to go to a wedding there today, only I took a wrong turn and I've spent the last hour driving in circles. Can you tell me where it is?"

A warm smile lit up his face. "I can do better than that. I'll take you there."

Suspicion reared its head again. Either this guy took small town friendliness to the ultimate degree, or he had an ulterior motive she didn't care to think about.

"That's not at all necessary. If you'll just—"

"You're Dove, aren't you?"

Alarm bells shrieked in her head. Her glance darted to the gas mart. She could see several people moving around inside. Safety in numbers. She'd lay on the horn, if it came to that. Someone would certainly come out. "How do you know my name?"

"Pennsylvania plate. Wedding at Shadow Lake." He ticked off the evidence on his fingers. "You couldn't be anyone else. Emma's been watching for you all morning. I'm Dusty," he said, thrusting his hand through her open window. "I'm a friend of Shane's."

•

Following the Escalade back up the winding road, she saw immediately where she'd made her mistake. The road was filled with precarious twists and unexpected jogs. At the third fork she'd mistakenly taken the right tine instead of the left, which had led her on a roundabout trek back into the city. A faint smile curved her lips and she thanked whatever whim of fate had sent Dusty to the gas mart at such an opportune moment.

With the remainder of the journey in his capable hands, she allowed herself to relax and enjoy the scenery. Gazing around her, she could understand why Emma had planned her wedding for the third week in October. The surrounding hillside was a symphony of colors—soft, muted yellows and oranges that built to a breathtaking crescendo of fiery reds and golds. The wedding pictures were going to be fabulous.

Fifteen minutes later she followed the Escalade into the parking lot at Shadow Lake Campground. Pulling into the first available spot, she climbed out of her car and smoothed the wrinkles from her dress.

"Head straight down that way," Dusty told her, indicating a wide, shady path. "About a hundred yards down you'll see a gazebo on your left. You can't miss it."

Rewarding him with a warm smile and a heartfelt "Thank you," she turned and hurried down the path.

The sun shone through the canopy of trees, creating a

patchwork of color all around her. Hollowed-out pumpkins in various sizes and shapes were scattered along the trail, serving as vases for autumn flowers in brilliant shades of crimson and gold. Ignoring the importunate electricity that hummed all around her, she breathed deeply of the pine-scented air, concentrating instead on the crunch of leaves beneath her feet and the twittering of birds high in the treetops. The campground was every bit as tranquil and as beautiful as Emma had promised, and Dove would be forever grateful for her friend's generosity. The invitation could not have come at a better time.

The Sarah Waterman investigation had shaken Dove to her very core. She'd been wrung out, an emotional wreck when Emma called from out of the blue to tell her about the upcoming wedding. Though they'd been out of touch for over a year, they'd talked for nearly an hour, picking up where they'd left off as if only days had passed.

"Anyway," Emma had finally said, "I know how busy you are with school and everything, Dove, but I'd love it if you could come for the wedding."

"Actually, Em, I'm taking a semester off."

"You are? Is everything okay?"

"Everything's fine. More or less. I'm just feeling a little unstrung right now."

"If you need a quiet place to regroup, you could come for the wedding and stay awhile. It's beautiful here. The foliage will take your breath away."

"That's sweet of you, Emma, but I don't want to intrude."

"Don't be s-silly. We have lots of guest cottages. With the campground closed for the season, they're just sitting empty. Promise you'll think about it, Dove. You could rest up, maybe write some of your articles."

And hide out, she thought. The hunt is on. She shivered, despite the warm October sun.

The path meandered through the woods, abruptly widening into a clearing where a small, white gazebo sat tucked among the trees, festooned with garlands of orange and rust-colored leaves. Forty or fifty guests sat in rows of folding chairs, chattering happily while classical music swelled from a boom box.

Dove slid into an empty chair in the back row with seconds to spare. Watching the groom approach the gazebo, she sucked in a breath. Broad shouldered and standing well over six feet tall, Shane Lucy was the embodiment of tall, dark and handsome. It was easy to see why Emma had fallen for him. He took his place beside a grinning young man sporting a silver lip ring and a green Mohawk. His son, Mick, Dove presumed. The boy's grin was infectious and Dove couldn't help but smile. Even in his suit and tie, he looked like a budding rock star.

Moments later the Wedding March began and Emma glided down the flower-strewn path, looking radiant in a pale peach gown, a chain of painted daisies in her hair. The honor of giving her away fell to Dusty, who stood tall and proud, his rough edges smoothed by a dark suit and tie. His gaze lingered on Dove as he passed, causing a surprising surge of warmth to flow through her.

Though not a blatantly good looking man, Dusty was a complex blend of roughness and gentleness that she found extremely appealing. Under different circumstances she might have pursued the attraction to see where it went. She wasn't averse to a little mutual physical gratification when the timing felt right. And the fact that she'd been given a glimpse into a dark corner of his past indicated their chemistry was compatible. But the timing was definitely not right. In fact, it couldn't have been more wrong, she thought, directing her attention back to the ceremony.

Shane and Emma had written their own vows and reciting her pledge, Emma's voice caught in a slight stutter, a telltale sign that she was nervous.

You can do it, Emma … Dove thought, sending positive energy her way.

A perfect reflection of Emma herself, the ceremony was simple, yet lovely. When it ended Dove took her place in the receiving line where Emma pulled her into a warm embrace. "Dove, I'm so glad you came."

"I'm sorry I was late, Em. I took a wrong turn and got lost."

"You're here now. That's all that m-matters." She turned to Shane, her face glowing. "Honey, this is my friend, Dove. Dove, meet Shane Lucy, my husband."

"I like the sound of that." His face broke into a warm smile. "It's great to finally meet you, Dove. Emma's told us a lot about you."

"And I've heard a lot about you." She clasped his outstretched hand. "Your campground is lovely, Shane. I appreciate your letting me stay."

He waved away her thanks. "It's my pleasure. Mick will take your things down to the cottage later and help you get settled in. Where'd he disappear to, anyway?"

"He's over behind the gazebo, flirting with Mrs. Donovan's niece."

Dove turned at the sound of Dusty's voice. Their eyes met and she smiled.

Shane rolled his eyes. "Now why doesn't that surprise me?"

"Dusty, this is my friend, D-dove," Emma said.

"We've met." He returned her smile, and she felt the uncomfortable warmth spread through her again.

"If you need anything at all while we're gone, Dusty is your man," Shane told her.

The photographer, a twenty-something man wearing baggy jeans and a row of silver hoops in his eyebrows appeared. "Yo, I don't mean to rush you two, but the light doesn't get much better than it is right now. Are you ready to do some pictures?"

While the wedding party gathered for photos on the steps of the gazebo, Dove moved with the other guests up the pathway to the rec hall, where she could already hear the sounds of music and celebration. Ahead of her, women crunched up the leaf-strewn path in high heels, chattering happily together, blissfully unaware of the electricity that crackled in the air.

Dove could feel them all around her, like persistent children tugging at her sleeve. So many voices, all of them desperate to be heard. Physically and emotionally depleted, she could not help them. She could not even help herself, and so she closed off her awareness of them. Effectively pushing them away, she continued on, idly wondering what Shane Lucy would think if he knew his campground was full of ghosts.

Chapter Two

By nine o'clock that evening the party was well on its way to over. The beer was flowing at a trickle, the band had graduated from classic rock to golden oldies, and Jane O'Dell was dancing on the tabletop.

Dusty smiled as she belted out an Elvis Presley hit, her forty-something hips swiveling in one of the best impersonations of the king he'd seen in awhile. A favorite among the permanent campers, Jane had a big heart and an even bigger predilection for fun. She'd worked tirelessly to help Emma organize the reception and she deserved to enjoy every moment of it. Dusty raised a glass of ginger ale in toast and she winked at him.

Shane and Emma had taken off hours before for a two-week honeymoon in Aruba. Since then, the day had been a blur of bodies, music, and loud voices. Dusty busied himself with keeping the buffet tables stocked and snapping candid photos for the campground's web site. He was more a nuts-and-bolts kind of man than a party animal, and besides that, seeing to the small details kept him from the temptation of alcohol. Four months sober, abstemiousness was a battle Dusty fought daily.

He sighed. It had been a long day all the way around, and he could feel the suggestion of a headache tiptoeing across the base of his skull. Weary of the clamor and clatter inside the rec hall, he stepped outside for a breath of cool evening air. Dove had evidently had her fill of the party, too. He'd seen her leave more than an hour ago. Shifting his gaze down the path in the direction of the guest cottages, he wondered whether it would be appropriate to walk down and see if she needed anything.

His stomach twisted at the thought of being alone with her. She was magnificent. The kind of woman Mick would have referred to as smokin' hot. Emma had told him Dove was lovely, but even so, Dusty had not been prepared for her beauty. With her dark, expressive eyes and her long, black hair she was like an exotic painting come to life, a wild and beautiful gypsy.

The moment he saw her come out of the gas mart Dusty knew she was special. Hoping to escape the buzz of female activity that filled the campground that morning, he'd gone to fill Shane and Emma's Escalade with gas for their drive to the airport. That Dove had been there at that exact moment he could attribute to nothing less than sheer good luck. And though he was attracted to her like he hadn't been attracted to a woman in years, he knew that in the give and take of male/female relationships, he had absolutely nothing to bring to the table. He was a handyman, unsophisticated and uneducated. He had no car. No home. He lived in a tent during summer, doing odd jobs around the campground. When cold weather set in, Shane brought him into his home, like a stray dog he felt sorry for.

Be that as it may, he had promised Emma he'd look after her friend while she was here. With this thought in mind, he started down the trail.

The guest cottages glowed eerily beautiful under the golden moon. For as long as he could remember they'd been crisp white, but at Emma's insistence, he and Mick had repainted them a misty rose color and trimmed them with glossy black shutters. Homey and inviting, they stood before him like something out of a Thomas Kincaid painting. Seeing a soft wash of light spilling from the window of cottage number four, he ran a hand through his hair, straightened his shoulders, and ambled toward it.

Stepping onto the porch, he tucked in his shirt before knocking at the door. When several moments passed with no response, he peered in the window. Two open suitcases lay in disarray on the sofa, while a candle flickered beside a bottle of wine on the coffee table. Across the room, the sliding door stood open and a breeze blew in off the lake, causing the curtains to flutter in the windows. Curious, he walked around to the back of the cottage, stopping abruptly when he heard her speaking.

Low and smoky, the ebb and flow of her voice told him she was speaking to someone on the phone. Her intimate tone told him it was someone special. He felt a pinprick of disappointment, acknowledged it, and then let it go. Knowing she was out of reach was a blessing. It would save him the sting of rejection that would surely have come had he entertained any romantic notions about Dove Denning. For as long as she was here, he'd enjoy her beauty like he enjoyed his morning ritual of rising early to watch the sun rise over Shadow Lake. Both breathtakingly lovely. Both absolutely unattainable.

Emma had said Dove would be staying in the cottage for a week or two but when Dusty questioned her further she was strangely evasive. Watching Dove's silhouette in the moonlight, he pieced together what he'd learned about the mysterious visitor.

He knew she was an instructor at a university in Philadelphia, and that she was in high demand as a lecturer on Paranormal studies. He also knew she worked with the Philadelphia police in some capacity to help solve murder cases, and that the last one had been particularly stressful and so she'd come to Shadow Lake to recuperate. Emma had also alluded to psychic abilities. Dusty didn't go in for a lot of hocus-pocus, for all of the strange magic that seemed to be so popular these days. Be that as it may, there was something he needed from Dove Denning.

Something he needed desperately.

•

The cottage was everything she'd hoped it would be; a secluded retreat situated at the edge of miles of clear, blue water. Inside, soothing cream colored walls trimmed in hunter green were offset by wide plank floors of weathered pine. An hour before, Shane's son, Mick, had been kind enough to help bring her belongings from the car. He was a friendly, outgoing boy with a mischievous quality about him that Dove found delightful. They chatted for a few moments about the wedding before he excused himself and returned to the party. When he'd gone, Dove plugged her cell phone into its charger and then spent some time investigating her surroundings.

Small and compact, the cottage consisted of three rooms and a bath. In the bedroom, a colorful and well used wedding ring quilt was turned down across a double bed. A bouquet of miniature sunflowers stood on the nightstand. The oversized bathroom was painted a tranquil blue, with an old fashioned tub and sink. A stack of fluffy white towels sat on the counter, and beside it a basket filled with sweet smelling soaps. She found the kitchen stocked with coffee, tea, and breakfast items. A bottle of wine chilled in a bucket on the counter. She smiled. Emma certainly knew how to make a person feel at home.

Opening the larger of her two suitcases, she pulled out her jeans and sweaters and stowed them in the bedroom closet, then, feeling restless, she poured a glass of wine and wandered out to the deck. The lake shimmered in the moonlight, dark and vast and luminous. She watched its slow, rippling movements as if hypnotized, and slowly felt the tension of the last few weeks begin to ease.

Hearing the muffled strains of Tchaikovsky, she hurried back inside, grabbed up her cell phone and answered the call. "Hello?"

"Hey."

She smiled. "Mark."

"I've been trying to get in touch with you for hours. How was your day?"

"Beautiful."

"So I'm assuming you made it there without any problems?"

"I had my moments."

"Got lost, huh?"

"Not lost, exactly. Just a little bit misplaced."

"Which is why I wanted you to take my GPS."

"You called to say I told you so?"

"No. I called to make sure you got there in one piece. I worry about you, Dove."

"I'm fine." She refilled her glass and wandered back outside.

"Why was your phone off?"

"The battery died."

He sighed. "You didn't notice anyone following you, did you?"

"No."

"Good. I'm working on a couple of possible leads, but I still don't have anything concrete yet, so be careful, alright?"

"I thought you said it was nothing to worry about."

"It probably isn't."

She chuckled softly. "You weren't this overprotective when we were married."

"No one threatened your life while we were married."

"I'll be careful, Mark."

After a pause, he said, "Is that a nice place out there?"

"It's heavenly. Peaceful, you know?"

"It sounds like just what you need right now."

"M-hmm."

"Listen, I gotta go. Erin's out at a baby shower and Izzy's bugging me for a bedtime story."

"Give her my love."

"Will do. Keep that battery charged up, okay?"

"Okay."

Ending the call, she stood at the railing and looked out at the nighttime sky. She considered the ever-watchful moon, keeping up its silent vigil for thousands of years, witnessing life in all its joy and sorrow and incomprehensibility. And she thought about Mark. Their marriage had been a disaster, and yet, she felt more connected to Mark Denning than to any other person on the face of the earth. Sipping her wine, she allowed herself a melancholy visit to the past.

She'd been a first-year instructor at the university when she and Mark met. At twenty-seven, she was already earning a reputation as an expert in the field of paranormal phenomena. A young detective at the end of his rope, Mark Denning had come to hear one of her lectures, and afterward had hung around to ask questions. He'd spent six months investigating the brutal murder of an elderly clairvoyant with every lead taking him down a dead-end road. With the DA's office breathing down his neck, he was feeling desperate. He'd heard she possessed certain insights and was hoping she could help. He was handsome and determined and he possessed a thirst for justice that matched her own. As the weeks passed, they worked tirelessly together on the investigation and Dove found herself falling in love. She and Mark were married a year later.

Their relationship had been stormy at best, but they shared a bond of mutual trust that held them together through it all. Until they found themselves faced with a hurdle they could not jump, fight out, or reason their way through.

They'd agreed early on not to have children. With Mark's monstrous work schedule, and Dove's family history of mental illness, the risks had seemed too great. Six years into their marriage, Mark changed the plan. At thirty-five, he began to burn with the desire for an offspring. At an impasse, they severed their marriage ties and went their separate ways.

Within a year, Mark remarried, and nine months later, the pair had a daughter. Young and optimistic, Erin Denning had provided what Dove wouldn't. With her own time clock marking off the days and the hours and the moments, it was a decision she'd recently come to regret.

A rustling in the leaves nearby startled her from her reverie and she stiffened as a figure emerged from the shadows.

"I'm sorry, did I scare you?" Dusty asked, stopping short.

She exhaled sharply. "Yes, actually you did. I thought you were some sort of wild animal."

He laughed softly. "Haven't been accused of that in a lot of years."

She smiled.

"I just came by to see if there was anything you needed."

"Not a thing. Emma seems to have taken care of everything."

"Good." He hesitated. "Then, I guess I'll leave you to settle in."

He looked as lonesome as she felt and just then the thought of his company was irresistible. "I was just enjoying a glass of wine and this marvelous view. Would you like to join me?"

He hesitated for just long enough that she thought he'd refuse, but then, shoving his hands in his pockets, he stepped up onto the deck and sat down in one of the two available chairs.

"Let me go and get you a glass."

Inside, she retrieved the wine bottle and a fresh goblet. Returning to the deck, she filled each of their glasses and sat down in the chair beside him. She breathed deeply of the crisp autumn air and the silence.

"Do you ever get used to this?"

"What's that?"

"The quiet."

He set his wine glass aside. "It becomes a way of life, after awhile."

"Have you lived here for a long time?"

"Long enough that I can barely remember a time I didn't."

She regarded him with curiosity, remembering again the vision she'd seen. "Tell me your story."

He chuckled. "Not much to tell, really. I left home when I was sixteen years old. David Lucy discovered me living in a tent on the edge of his campground and put me to work. I've more or less been here ever since."

"You left home at sixteen?"

"Yeah."

"Why?"

He shrugged. "I don't even remember anymore."

But something in his eyes told her differently. Something sad and far away that said he bore the scars of abuse, just as she did. *Oh, but you do remember. Don't you?*

"So, how do you know Emma?" he asked, neatly changing the subject.

She took a slow sip from her goblet. "I met Emma when she was a sophomore at the university where I teach. She took my class that year as an elective." She smiled. "Most attentive student I've ever had, and probably one of the brightest. She stayed to talk almost every day after class. We've been friends ever since."

"You teach history, right?"

"What makes you think that?"

"Emma mentioned that you write articles about old buildings."

"That's part of my research. Actually, I'm an instructor in paranormal studies."

"You mean ghosts?"

"Among other things."

A few tense moments passed. Dove sensed Dusty had something to say, but whatever it was, it remained unspoken.

Finally, he stood. "I should be getting back."

"Thanks for coming to check on me."

"My pleasure." He shifted, obviously ill at ease, and finally blurted, "Do you have any plans for tomorrow, Dove? The reason I ask is that there's a ski resort not too far from here. This time of year a lot of people like to go up on the chair lifts and check out the foliage. I think you might enjoy it."

"That sounds lovely. But please don't feel you have to baby sit me while I'm here. I'm sure you're busy."

"Actually, I've been wanting to make the trip. There's a neat old tavern nearby the slopes, built in the 1800s, I think. We could have lunch there. Maybe you could write a story about it some day."

"I'd like that, Dusty."

"Good, then. How about if I stop by for you around ten?"

"I'll be ready."

When he left, Dove gathered up her empty wine glass, along with Dusty's full one and carried them into the cottage. In the bathroom, she slipped out of her dress and pulled on a flannel nightgown. She washed her face, brushed her hair, and headed back to the living room, yawning. A night of driving and a day of festivity had finally caught up with her. Sleep would come easily this night.

Crossing the room to pull the curtains closed, she froze when she saw a figure standing on the dock; a young girl in a black bathing suit. Her skin was milky white, her hair long and untamed. Dove pulled in a breath. *Don't get involved ...*

She closed her eyes, exhaled softly. When she opened them again, the girl was still there, regarding her pensively with her dark, shadowy eyes.

Don't ... Ignoring her inner voice, Dove slid open the door and stepped outside. She stood without speaking, her gaze locked with that of the specter.

You can see me? The girl finally asked.

Yes.

None of the others can.

What do you want?

I want... I want you to tell him I'm sorry. Please?

Who?

She choked on a sob. *My dad.*

Who are you?

Silence fell like a thick, dark veil. The ghost drew closer. Shivering in her nightgown, Dove braced herself against a blast of frigid air, against the sheer, raw strength of the emotions that swirled like a cyclone inside the girl. Images exploded in her brain, one after another: a small girl splashing in the water, running with a jar of lightning bugs, riding piggy back high on a man's shoulders. She watched as each impression gave way to the next, as the pretty little girl became a lovely young woman. She saw her competing at a high school swim meet as a crowd of onlookers cheered, dancing in a lavender gown, a string of pearls around her pretty neck, riding a ten speed bike, her hair dancing in the wind. And then came a final, horrible image. A blood-curdling scream as she plunged head first into the icy lake, her hands groping blindly in terror and confusion as the water closed in around her.

Dove nearly buckled beneath the force of its fury as the specter fought to gain entry into her being. Summoning her inner strength, she steeled herself against the onslaught until she felt its energy begin to weaken. Its fervor lessened and then disappeared, leaving only a whispered breath of air in its wake.

I'm Chelsea ...

Trembling, sweating profusely, she stumbled back inside and closed the door. Standing beneath the hot spray of the shower, she tried to rid herself of the images the girl had shown her, and of the memories of Sarah Waterman they had unleashed. Another young girl. Another wasted life. Another desperate request.

Tell him I'm sorry.

But she couldn't. Not this time. She was too depleted, too much of an emotional wasteland. *This is how it happens*, she thought. *This is how the gifted go insane.*

She felt a familiar twinge of fear and reminded herself she was not like her mother. She was stronger. Smarter. Certainly smart enough to know when to walk away. She would not involve herself with Chelsea, whoever she was. She would go back to Philadelphia and take her chances with the more corporeal danger of a stalker.

Opening her suitcase, she pulled out her toothbrush and another clean nightgown. Leaving the suitcase on the sofa, she returned to the bathroom to dress for bed. She wouldn't bother to unpack the rest of her things. She'd be leaving first thing in the morning.

Chapter Three

It was a vicious cycle. The more Dusty tried not to think about her, the more she seemed to fill his mind. He pulled back gently on the oars, smoothly propelling his boat through the silent water. Above him, the morning sky gently exploded into color; red fading to violet, fading to pink. He turned his collar up against the cold, gazing across the lake, allowing its tranquility to fill him. Morning on the lake. His favorite time of day.

He'd started the ritual four months earlier, when Mick's suicide attempt had caused him to rethink his own existence. It made him realize he wanted not merely to exist, but to live. And what was life but a succession of moments, each one to be savored and enjoyed for as long as it lasted. The sunrise mornings were a time to exercise his body, but more than that, a time to quiet his spirit. Dusty did his best thinking in these predawn moments, when he set his boat and his mind adrift, allowing them to wander where they pleased. Today his thoughts rambled back to the exact place he'd left them the night before. To Dove Denning.

He lay awake for most of the night thinking of her hair, her eyes, and the velvet sound of her voice. He found himself looking cautiously forward to the day ahead, much as he'd looked forward to birthdays when he was small; knowing they would end in disappointment, but still, allowing himself to hope for the best. Now, as it had then, a small inner voice warned that he was setting himself up. He was letting it mean too much to him. Gazing in the direction of her cottage, he reminded himself there was a chance she couldn't help him. And even if she could, there was no guarantee that she would.

Back on shore, he tethered the boat to the dock and propelled himself up the path to begin phase two of his morning ritual. Removing a good sized chunk of black walnut from the pile by the woodshed, he arranged it on the chopping block, picked up his maul and swiftly brought it down, neatly splitting the wood in half.

He reached for another, echoes of last evening's conversation with Dove reverberating in his mind. Tell me your story, she'd said. As if it mattered anymore.

He swung the maul again, sending pieces of splintered wood skittering into the pile. No, his childhood didn't matter anymore. It was years ago, another lifetime. Call it shame, or better, a recrudescence of his battered pride. He hadn't felt the need to share that piece of his life with Dove, to expose to her the undersized, abused boy he'd once been.

Even a small, wealthy city like Hope Haven had its dark corners and Dusty's family had inhabited the bleakest of them. He'd grown up in filth and poverty in a three-room duplex on Bolton Street. As a child, he and his brothers had spent most of their time outdoors, swimming in the river and playing kickball on the broken sidewalks, the possible dangers of the Southside streets being preferable to the certain punishment that awaited them at home. Like his brothers, Dusty never questioned his father's beatings. He endured the drunken rages as if they were as natural a part of childhood as summertime and the county fair. At sixteen his father finally threw him out and the Lucys took him in, treated him like a son. They were the closest thing to a real family he'd ever had, until he created his own. Thoughts of his beautiful, raven-haired daughter intruded and he felt a stab of pain.

He'd had the perfect opportunity to ask Dove last night and in the end he couldn't do it. If it turned out she couldn't help him, the disappointment would have been too great.

Maybe today, the inner voice whispered.

The wood pile depleted, he headed inside, took a hot shower, and changed into clean jeans and a shirt. He entered the kitchen to find Mick sitting at the breakfast table.

"You're up early."

Mick shrugged. "Couldn't sleep."

Dusty retrieved a coffee cup from the drain board. "I thought I might make some omelets this morning. Sound good?"

"Thanks, dude, but I already got it covered."

He inspected the smudges of pink and blue that smeared Mick's plate. "Wedding cake?"

Mick grinned. "Breakfast of champions."

"I'm supposed to be supervising you. Somehow I don't think Miss Emma would approve."

"Yeah, but Miss Emma ain't here."

"Since you put it that way … Any cake left?"

"Tons."

Opening the fridge, he cut a generous slice of cake and carried it back to the table. He and Mick talked about the wedding, and about Mrs. Donovan's niece, Candy. Finally Mick stood.

"I better hit the shower. Do you mind if I take the truck to town later?"

Dusty hesitated. "It'll have to be a lot later. I have somewhere I have to go. Do you have plans with Candy today?"

Mick snorted. "In my dreams. I was just gonna hang out with Boots for awhile, but if you're doing something more interesting, maybe I'll go with you."

"Well …" he hesitated again. "The thing is, Mick …"

A slow smile spread across Mick's face. "Dude, have you got a date with Miz Denning?"

"It's not a date. It's an outing."

His smile widened. "Sweet."

"We're going to drive up to Crystal Mountain to view the foliage. You're welcome to come along."

"Naw, dude. I'd feel mad out of place. I'll send Boots a text. Maybe he'll come and pick me up."

Despite Dusty's weak stab at protest, Mick flipped open his cell phone, his fingers working the key pad.

Dusty stacked the dishes in the dishwasher, then wiped down the counters and swept the floor clean. He glanced at the clock. Five minutes to ten. With no more putting it off, he walked down the path in the direction of Dove's cottage.

•

It wasn't a headache. It was more of an explosion. Dove lay in bed, trying to ignore the insistent hammering that started in her head and seemed to echo in the air around her. The conflict with Chelsea had taken a lot out of her. A lot more than it should have.

She'd gone to bed with a headache blooming behind her eyes, craving sleep, only to have that fragile state shattered again and again by nightmares of Sarah Waterman. She'd been tortured by visions in which she'd seen the inferno, felt the raging heat, the sheer terror of smoke clogging her lungs. She'd awakened slick with sweat, every muscle knotted and aching. At six a.m. she'd shed her soaked nightgown, fumbled in her bag for a bottle of Excedrin, and stumbled back to bed, awakening what seemed moments later to the sound of persistent pounding at the cottage door. Opening her eyes, she glanced at the bedside clock. Her head shrieked with pain.

"Ten o'clock," she murmured. With the words came the slow realization that she had a date with Dusty Martin.

"Damn," she whispered.

Easing herself from the bed, she wrapped herself in her robe and went to answer the door. Dusty's face creased with worry, telling her she looked as bad as she felt.

"What's wrong?" he asked.

"I'm sorry, Dusty. I'm not going to be able to go today."

"What's wrong?" he repeated.

"I feel like there's an elephant sitting on my head."

"Migraine?"

"Uh-huh."

"I can help."

Help. The word brought a surge of hope. Disregarding her tangled hair, her swollen eyes, and the fact that she was barely dressed, she stepped aside to let him in.

His gaze swept across the room. "Have you got any lotion?"

"I think there's some in my bag." She gestured toward the sofa, a gesture which sent a stab of pain crashing through her brain.

"Go and lie down," he said, rummaging in her overnight bag.

If some deep seated sense of politesse told her a man she barely knew should not be in her bedroom, Dove ignored it. Obeying his request, she pushed back the twisted knot of blankets and lay down on her stomach.

"Try and relax."

He crossed the room and closed the curtains before approaching the bed. He tugged on her robe and she slid her arms out of it, letting it fall to the floor as he uncapped a bottle of lavender scented lotion and worked it through his hands. Pushing her hair out of the way, he went to work. His hands glided over her skin, kneading the muscles of her neck and shoulders; applying deep pressure here, a whisper soft touch there. She felt an immediate easing of the pain and groaned with relief.

As he worked, she gave in to the pleasure of his touch, savored the magic his hands wrought as they manipulated each muscle and tendon. It was one of the most sensuous things she'd ever experienced. She'd resisted sleep in the night, afraid of the visions, the night fears, but now she felt inexplicably protected. She didn't know Dusty Martin, but oddly, she trusted him, and beneath his watchful eye, she let herself drop gently into sleep.

•

He'd performed the massage more than a hundred times in the sixteen years he'd been married to Colleen, and though he hadn't done it in more than eight years, his hands knew the routine by heart. They knew instinctively where to apply pressure, where to tread lightly. As Dusty settled into a rhythm, he found his thoughts rambling to dangerous places. Dove's skin was exquisite; warm and supple, a treat to touch. He studied the mole on her left shoulder, the fading tan lines that suggested a piece of tantalizing swimwear. Black, he wondered. Red? He felt the fierce ache of longing and was glad she wasn't able to see his face, certain it was spelled out there in no uncertain terms.

Fear and desire, he thought. His lifelong companions.

A glimmer of a memory surfaced. Nearly three decades had passed since then, and it surprised him how sharply the memory still cut him. So sharply that the years seemed to fall away and once again he was that small, scruffy boy standing outside the fence.

It was May and the carnival was in town. He watched the lights along the midway twinkle red, green and gold, his heart pounding with the vicarious thrill of watching those more fortunate dip and soar as the Magic Dragon made it clattering way over the ramps. His mouth watered at the scents of grilled Italian sausage and sugar waffles. He would have given anything to ride that ride, to taste the powdery sweetness of the confections, to be standing on the other side of the fence. But the three-dollar cost of the ticket that would make that happen was an insurmountable obstacle, and so he remained ever the outsider.

As the evening sun began to set, he noticed a group of boys he knew from school walking toward him. One of them was Kyle Marlin. Their fifth grade teacher, Mrs. Fennell, arranged her students alphabetically, which put Kyle in the seat directly ahead of Dusty. Kyle and Dusty had an unspoken agreement; Dusty would give him the answers to his math problems, and in return Kyle would share with Dusty from his lunch box. And if they weren't exactly friends, at least Kyle didn't torment him like the other playground bullies.

Seeing Kyle approaching, Dusty's heart swelled with hope. Kyle's parents were rich, and had undoubtedly sent their son off to the carnival with plenty of money. Maybe Kyle would spot him the three bucks. He wouldn't ask. He had too much pride. But maybe Kyle would offer.

He stuffed his hands in his pocket, trying hard to look nonchalant. "Hey, Kyle."

"Hey, Dusty. You going in?"

He shrugged, swiftly losing his nerve. "I might."

He'd foolishly thought the others would accept him based on his tenuous friendship with Kyle, but all his hopes were dashed when one of the boys in the group called out to him.

"Hey, guys, look at the welfare rat, slinking around the fence."

"Nice pants, Noah," another chimed in. "When's the flood?"

Laughter rang out, mingling with the sounds of carnival music and barking food vendors. Kyle didn't join in, but he also did nothing to defend Dusty.

"You wanna come in, welfare rat?" the boy shrieked. "Tell your old man to get a job!"

Still laughing, they walked past, leaving Dusty alone with his shame.

Sighing softly, he let the memory fade away. The incident was too many years ago to matter, but its lesson was hard learned. Knowing the end result would likely be similar, he tore his eyes from Dove's lovely body, forcing himself to concentrate on what he was doing, rather than what he'd like to do.

He continued to make low, gentle circles on her back long after she slept, savoring the sensation of being in bed with beautiful woman. Well, not exactly in bed, but as close as he'd come in longer than he cared to remember. He massaged her until his fingers were numb, then covered her with the sheet and left, quietly closing the door behind him.

When he returned to the cabin it was almost noon and Mick was back into the cake.

"You're back already?" he asked, shooting a glance at the clock.

"We didn't go."

"Why not?"

"She's got a migraine."

"That's too bad," he said around a forkful of frosting.

"No big deal." Dusty tossed the key ring on the table. "I guess you can go ahead and take the truck."

"Boots isn't gonna be around. His sister came home from college for Homecoming weekend. He's taking her back today."

"You didn't want to go along?" Dusty asked, grabbing a kaiser roll and a package of sliced ham from the fridge. "Meet some college girls?"

"Hell yeah I wanted to go along." Mick drained his milk glass and poured another. "But with all the crap-o-la she brought there wasn't enough room in the car."

"Ahh." He sliced the roll, added a generous dollop of mayo, and arranged the ham on top.

"What are you going to do now?" Mick asked.

"There's a walnut tree out in woods that need to be bucked up. I guess I might as well get at it."

"I'll go with you."

Dusty regarded him in surprise. "Your dad told me to give you the day off today."

Mick shrugged and cut another wedge of cake.

Later that afternoon, chainsaws buzzing, Dusty and Mick worked at the limbs of the enormous old tree. They worked in tee shirts, despite the crisp autumn air, stopping intermittently to guzzle ice water and wipe the streams of sweat from their faces. They took advantage of the quiet moments, chatting about the campground's recent season and all the changes that had come about at Shadow Lake since Emma's arrival.

"It always seems weird in October, when no one's around," Mick commented. "I sort of like having the place to ourselves."

"Don't speak too soon." Dusty said, his eyes trained on the man walking toward them. He was forty, give or take a year, short and solidly built, but obviously out of shape, panting with the exertion of the hike. His overgrown hair, a good seven days' stubble of beard, and dirty jeans stood in sharp contrast to the expensive camera slung around his neck. It bounced against his chest as he walked.

"Help you?" Dusty said, as the man drew nearer.

"How are ya? Name's Paul Peters," he said, and Dusty detected a slight southern inflection. The man extended a hand and Dusty shook it. He'd always thought you could tell a lot about a man from his handshake. The one he now grasped was weak, definitely not a working man's hand.

"I'm a freelance writer and photographer," the man said, indicating the camera. "I was hoping to get some shots of your lake with the foliage at its peak. I'll credit the campground in my article, of course."

Shane often allowed hikers to use the trails after season, saying it was good public relations, but there was something about Paul Peters that put Dusty on edge, something he couldn't quite nail down.

"The campground's closed for the season. Including the trails."

The man's smile slipped. "I'm sorry. I didn't know."

Avoiding Mick's eyes, Dusty took a swig of water. He picked up his chainsaw, hoping Peters would take the hint and leave.

"I'd really like to get those shots. I'd be happy to pay for a day pass."

"We don't offer day passes after season."

Something cold and hard flashed in his eyes. "Can't you bend the rules just this once?"

Dusty met his gaze unflinchingly. "Fraid not."

Glaring, he turned and stalked back down the trail, Dusty and Mick watching after him.

"Why didn't you want him up here?" Mick finally asked.

"I don't know." He capped his bottle. "I think we've done enough for today. Let's load up and head back."

A half hour later, with the fruits of their afternoon's labor piled in the back of the truck, Dusty and Mick headed home. They stacked the wood neatly on the woodpile and went inside. In the kitchen, Mick opened the fridge and took out the cake.

"Dinner of champions?" Dusty asked.

"This is just a snack," Mick told him, cutting a generous wedge.

"It's after five. I was going to grill some hamburgers."

"We can just make sandwiches, if you want. There's mad cold cuts left over from yesterday."

"Suit yourself. I'm going to go and get cleaned up," he said, heading down the hallway.

"After that you should go and check on Ms. Denning," Mick called from behind him.

Dusty turned back. "She's probably resting."

"Yeah, but if she doesn't feel good she may not want to go out and get dinner. You should take her something later."

Of course he should. It would be the decent thing to do, the responsible thing. The uncomfortable thing. He thought of her skin and of his body's violent reaction to her touch. Walking into the bathroom, he stripped off his clothes, turned on the shower, and adjusted the water to cool.

After a brisk clean-up he returned to the kitchen. Uncomfortable or not, he wanted to see her, and for reasons that had nothing to do with his attraction to her. He needed help and didn't know where else to get it. Grabbing a meat tray from the refrigerator, he arranged slices of beef, ham, and Swiss cheese on a platter. Completing his creation with kaiser rolls and a selection of fruit, he shoved it in a grocery sack and made his way back down the path.

The cottage was quiet and dark. Realizing she might still be sleeping, Dusty debated whether to knock and risk disturbing her, or to leave the grocery sack on the porch and just go. But that would be foolish. The moment he left, some hungry animal would make a feast of it. Shifting the sack to his hip, he rapped softly on the door. If she didn't answer the first knock, he'd leave.

He heard the sound of footsteps approaching and then the door opened and Dove stood before him, dressed in a pair of rose-colored jogging pants and a matching hoodie. Even with her haphazard braid and puffy eyelids, she was stunning.

"Feeling better?" he asked.

"Much."

"Good." They regarded each other for a moment. "I didn't know if you'd be hungry."

"I'm starved. Actually, I was just thinking about venturing to town."

"I saved you the trip," he said, handing her the bag.

"Thank you very much."

"My pleasure."

"Have you eaten?"

"No."

"Will you join me?"

She stood aside to let him enter. In the center of the coffee table, a pale blue candle flickered, scenting the air with a sweetly exotic perfume.

"That's nice," he said. "What is it?"

"It's called Morning Sky. I find it very soothing. Please, sit."

He perched on the edge of the sofa while she moved around in the kitchen. Opening the bag, he removed the platter and set it on the coffee table.

"Would you like a drink?" she called.

"Water would be great."

She returned with two plates and two glasses of water. Setting them on the table, she surveyed the feast. "This is so thoughtful of you, Dusty."

He liked the way his name dropped gently from her lips. "It's no problem."

They composed thick ham sandwiches and piled their plates with fruit. Settling back on the sofa, they dug in with gusto, not speaking again until they'd finished the meal. He liked watching her eat, liked the way she relished every bite, as if the meal were a celebration. He liked the way her tongue flicked out to catch a dab of mustard that rested tantalizingly on her lip. God… Who'd have thought watching a woman eat a sandwich could be so arousing? Finally, she wiped her mouth with a napkin and turned her eyes on him, her beautiful, Gypsy eyes. "I can't thank you enough for this morning. That massage. It was incredible. How did you know what to do?"

"My wife used to get migraines. We tried every cure known to man. Pills. Herbs. Chiropractors. We finally went to see a massage therapist. She taught me the technique."

She regarded him thoughtfully. "I didn't know you were married."

A bite of cantaloupe stuck in his throat.

He'd been wandering aimlessly through his life, working when he had to and drinking when he could afford to, when Colleen took him up. With her charismatic personality and bubbling laughter, she was effervescent, if not pretty. She set her sights on him, organized him, like a pet project. She straightened out his life, gave him a dream for the future. Young and aimless, he'd allowed her to steer their lives, and with Colleen at the helm, he never doubted for a moment their ship would stay the course.

They'd been happy together, if not prosperous, creating a home and a family, and for Dusty, that was enough. But when they'd lost Chelsea it was as if someone had pulled a plug, and all of Colleen's years of hard work went down the drain in an instant.

It wouldn't have been fair to say that Colleen left him. He'd driven her away, ignoring her need for comfort and shunning her attempts to give it. He started drinking incessantly, desperate for a reprieve from his pain and guilt. Their marriage ended six months to the day after Chelsea died. He often wondered where life had taken Colleen, and whether she'd found happiness.

Dove watched him intently, waiting for an answer, and he allowed his memories of Colleen to fade away. "I'm not."

Though it was another unflattering piece of his past he'd rather not expose, he prepared himself for questions, gathering the courage to blurt out the whole, excruciating story. It would be the perfect opportunity to ask for her help. If only he could find the nerve.

She regarded him for a long moment. He was equally relieved and disappointed when she changed the subject. "You learned well. I've spent a fortune in the last year on cures. That massage was better than all of them put together."

"You've been getting the headaches for a year?"

"M-hmm." She took a sip of water. "My mother used to get migraines. She couldn't bear the least bit of noise. My brother and I used to tiptoe around the house, terrified of disturbing her. We always felt like we were walking around land mines. Sometimes the headaches lasted for days. When they came, we knew she was getting sick again."

"Sick," he echoed.

"She was insane," she said simply. "Of course, we didn't know that at the time. We just knew she wasn't like our friends' mothers. Unpredictable. It kept us on edge."

"Sounds like a tough way to grow up."

"I went to live with my grandmother when I was thirteen, when the family finally caught on to how bad it was. They put my mother in an institution. My brother had left home by then."

"I'm sorry," he murmured, unable to formulate a more suitable response.

"I've spent my whole life being afraid the same thing would happen to me."

He glanced at her in surprise. "Why would it?"

She paused, as if on the cusp of a revelation, and then shrugged delicately. "Genetics. Stress."

"Maybe you should find less stressful work."

She smiled, but it didn't quite reach her eyes. "It's not what I do. It's what I am."

His pulse quickened. It was coming.

"I see things sometimes, people."

A sheen of sweat broke out on his forehead. *Ask her*, the inner voice demanded. He cleared his throat. "You mean people who have died?"

"Yes."

His pulse pounded in his ears and for a moment he couldn't breathe. "Have you seen anyone here?"

"No."

But she had. He could feel it in the tense moments before she answered, see it in the way her eyes dropped away from his. It was in the way she stood and abruptly began to clear away the plates.

"Anyway, thanks again. For today," she said, heading to the kitchen.

With a sense of panic, he felt the opportunity slipping away, like a vessel tossed in a raging sea, no way to steer it back on course.

"I'm sorry I spoiled our plans to go leaf-peeping. Can we go tomorrow?"

"I'm going to be busy most of the day." He stood, feeling faint, the room spinning around him. His hands tightened into fists and he jammed them in his pockets for fear he'd grab her and shake the truth out of her. "I'd better be getting back."

He beat a hasty retreat from the cottage, hurrying up the path, welcoming the cool evening air on his burning skin. There wasn't a doubt in his mind she'd lied, and the implications were devastating. It went against everything he'd ever believed, confirmed what he'd sensed, mornings out on the lake. What he'd told himself couldn't be true.

His daughter was still here. Dove Denning had seen her.

Chapter Four

On Monday afternoon Dove sat with her head bent over her laptop, a menagerie of notes and photographs spread out on the table around her. She'd been working for hours, and when a commotion on the lake drew her attention to the window, she welcomed the distraction.

She watched with interest as a motorboat cut a frothy path across the water. A silver-haired man in jeans and a sweatshirt navigated the boat, while a woman wearing a bright red scarf and a pair of oversized sunglasses sat in the passenger seat. Tanned and fit, they represented everything a couple's golden years should be and Dove envied their easy camaraderie, and the comfort of a relationship that had likely spanned decades.

The knowledge that she'd missed out on such a relationship brought a pang of loneliness and she firmly pushed it away. She'd never been one to second-guess her decisions, let alone waste time feeling sorry for herself and she could only wonder at the vague, unsettled feeling that surfaced more and more often lately, whispering that time was running out. There was so much she'd hoped to accomplish, and more and more she felt the weight of things undone sitting heavy on her shoulders. Chalking the feeling up to some sort of mid-life crisis, she turned back to her work.

Before long a dull, burning sensation began between her shoulder blades. Lifting her hands to massage the base of her neck, she skimmed over the pages she'd written.

Satisfied that it was a good day's work, she saved the document and switched off her laptop with a sense of satisfaction.

She'd mentioned to Dusty that she wrote articles about old buildings, but that was only part of it. The truth was she was compiling a book about her experiences with the spirit world. She'd been playing at it for years, never finding the time to put her scribbled notes in any kind of order. Until now. Contemplating her options over breakfast that morning, she'd decided the opera house story would be the perfect opening chapter. Digging out the notes and the photographs she'd taken earlier that summer, she was happy to find them every bit as fascinating now as they'd been four months earlier.

When she received an anonymous email back in June about strange occurrences in the small Mississippi town she'd been intrigued enough to make the thousand-mile journey south. At first glance the village had seemed like any small town in America with its shady trees, well kept houses, and a business district consisting of gas stations, beauty shops, and family-run diners. Not the sort of place where extraordinary things happened, until recently. Upon questioning the town's residents, Dove immediately grasped the situation: overturned porch furniture, doorbells ringing in the night, traffic lights blinking red and green simultaneously, all within weeks of the demolition of the Warner Hotel. There wasn't a doubt in her mind the building had been haunted.

From what she gathered from reading the historical documents in the town library, the opera house had been the village hub at the turn of the century, hosting school spelling bees, local talent shows, and plays put on by traveling theater groups. Built in the eighteen-hundreds, the grand old structure was on the cutting edge of architecture for its time, with a hotel occupying the two lower floors, while the third floor contained a dance hall and opera house.

Ill-fated from start, the building had seen more than its share of tragedies: a half-dozen hotel guests who mysteriously died in their beds, the murder of a visiting actress, and the eventual suicide of the hotel's owner in 1904. It changed hands five times in as many decades, until, partially destroyed by a kitchen fire, the old hotel was boarded up in 1955. Year after year, an anxious town planning board petitioned the state for funds to restore the local landmark, but to no avail. After sitting vacant for more than fifty years, the building was finally condemned and torn down, effectively displacing its ghosts. There were six of them that Dove knew of. Simply put, they were madder than hell.

She'd been working on the story when the Sarah Waterman investigation started and the case had so fully consumed her she hadn't thought about the small Mississippi town in months. If nothing else, her brief sabbatical at Shadow Lake would give her time to finish writing the story.

With a good chunk of that task completed, she put away her notes and wandered back to the window. The afternoon sun sparkled on the lake, while a gentle breeze played with the leaves of the red Maples that lined the hiking trails. Feeling restless, she grabbed her parka from the bedroom closet and set off toward the beach.

The rhythm of the waves lapping at the sand was hypnotic and Dove felt more in tune with herself with every step she took. The wide, blue sky stretched out above her and she savored the absence of city noise; traffic, police sirens, people tripping over one another as they rushed about their lives.

She'd walked for nearly an hour when she came upon an abandoned building, its windows broken and its sun-scorched paint a faded yellow. Above the door a washed out sign swayed gently in the breeze. Squinting at it, she could just make out the words *Jerry's Bait and Tackle Shoppe.* A rusted bench sat neglected on a broken slab of concrete beside the front door and she sat down to rest.

She rested for a long moment, enjoying the sunshine and the quiet until an almost imperceptible humming sound drew her eyes back to the building. A pair of tattered curtains stirred as a breeze blew through the broken window, carrying with it the echo of a man's voice. Her hands began to tingle as a current of energy swirled in the air around her, carrying with it residual traces of anger and fear. Sensing movement, she glanced left at the dock, where a German shepherd paced back and forth, his eyes trained expectantly on the lake. She regarded him thoughtfully, taking in the aura that surrounded him. Pale pink. The color of unconditional love. Noticing her, he stopped pacing and stood, taking her in with his sorrowful eyes.

What happened here, boy?

A low growl started deep in his throat and built to a mournful howling. His gaze lingered for a moment on the building behind her, and then he vanished before her eyes.

All at once her senses were ambushed by a series of images; a harvest moon, a pocket watch, a red can filled with gasoline. Her mouth went dry and her heart fluttered with fear. She searched the building for evidence of a fire and found none. She struggled to catch her breath as the images came at her faster, slamming against her like waves pounding the shore. Breathing deep, she reached inside herself until she found her center of tranquility. She grabbed hold of it, holding on for dear life until the images began to fade. When they died away completely, she rose from the bench and started back the way she'd come. Glancing over her shoulder, she saw that the German shepherd had reappeared to resume his faithful vigil and Dove wondered what ugly secrets lay hidden beneath water's calm veneer.

The thought sparked a flame of anger inside her and she started to run. Why did the ugliness have to invade her life? How she wished she could be free of the visions. How she wished she could enjoy a simple moment without phantoms creeping up on her unawares. They came to her like songs across the airwaves, sometimes faint and static-filled, and sometimes with startling clarity. The second sight. The gift and curse of generations of Christiano women before her.

As she ran, she pondered the negative energy emanating from the bait and tackle shop, the visions she'd seen, so different in their feel and urgency from the others, and she couldn't help but wonder at their meaning. *Don't think about it. Don't let it in.* She slowed to a walk, breathed in, breathed out. *Don't let it win.*

An hour later she returned to her cottage, her earlier happiness evaporated. Opening the fridge, she grabbed the last of the bottled water Emma had left for her. As she guzzled it down, her gaze swept over the contents of the shelves, taking inventory. An egg. A half a croissant. A bowl of fruit. She'd have to drive into town and pick up some supplies. Glancing at her watch, she saw that it was well after four o'clock. Better get moving. It would be dark soon, and she didn't want to chance getting lost again. With a sigh, she scribbled out a shopping list, grabbed up her purse, and headed out the door, locking it behind her.

When she reached the parking lot, she noticed Mick sitting on the front porch of the cabin. He was listening to an ipod, and when he saw her, he waved and removed his earphones.

"Hi, Mick."

"Hey, Ms. Denning." He stood and ambled toward her. "Do you happen to know where Dusty went?"

"I haven't seen him all day."

"Oh." His glance rested on the car keys in her hand. "Are you going somewhere?"

"I have to run to the grocery store."

"Do you mind if I catch a ride to town with you?"

"Actually, Mick, that would be great. I haven't driven out here after dark before. You can be my personal navigation system."

"Cool. Let me just leave Dusty a note."

He sprinted inside, returning moments later. When he'd settled himself in the passenger seat, Dove steered the Impala out of the lot and down the winding road.

"It really sucks not having a car," he told her. "For one thing, I have to ride the school bus and that bites."

"I'm sure."

"If Dusty's using the truck when I get home, I pretty much have to stay there. Emma said she'd talk to my dad about getting me a car of my own."

"That would be nice."

He snorted. "It would be a freaking miracle, is what it would be. Dad says I have to wait until I'm eighteen. But Miss Emma, she's got a way of softening him up."

Dove smiled.

"I've been doing some reconnaissance. You know, just in case."

Her smile widened. "Reconnaissance?"

"Yeah. I found a really sweet Mustang convertible. A '97 Cobra. Five grand, and all it needs is new paint. Well, and maybe a tranny, but me and dad could spank that in a weekend."

He kept up a steady stream of chatter all the way into town, extolling the virtues of the Mustang. His youthful optimism stood in sharp contrast to the gloom that seemed to have settled over her and she found herself enjoying his company immensely. When they reached the city limits, his train of conversation abruptly shifted gears.

"I need to go to a place called The Video Café. It's on the corner of First and Peach Streets, up ahead, about three blocks on your left."

Following his directions, she pulled into the lot and shifted the car into Park.

"You don't have to wait. Go do your shopping and pick me up afterwards."

"Are you sure, Mick? I might be gone for quite awhile."

"That's ok," he said, grinning. "There's a girl that works here I sort of like. I'll just hang out and talk to her until you get back." He slid out of the passenger's seat, and as she put the car in gear, he called, "Hey, do you like horror flicks?"

"I don't know. I've never seen one." Not on film, anyway.

"Get outta here! You've never seen a horror flick?"

"Uh-uh."

"Oh, man, are you in for a sweet treat. Since Halloween's not too far off I'm going to rent *Nightmare on Elm Street*. It's a classic. You gotta come over and watch it with me later."

•

Dusty had run every errand on his list. He'd dropped the flyers for the Halloween party off at the printers and stopped by the newspaper office with the ad copy. He'd ordered the new part for the dishwasher and picked up a chain for his saw. He'd gone to an AA meeting. He'd done everything he could possibly think of to avoid being at the campground with Dove. And it was only Monday.

For months after he quit drinking, Dusty dreamed of alcohol. He'd awaken in a sheen of sweat, half out of his mind with cravings, with the desire for just a taste. The alcohol dreams were hell. The Dove Denning dreams were worse.

In last night's version they sailed together on a clear, blue ocean. Seagulls circled in the sky above, while bottomless blue waves rocked them gently from beneath. Dove sat beside him, the sun on her face and the wind caressing her hair like a lover. Grinning, she dipped her fingers into the water and splashed him. He caught her hands up in his. Laughing, she wrapped her arms around him and kissed him, and the kiss seemed to last forever ...

He awakened from the dream with a tempest of emotions raging inside him, feelings of anger complicated by his undeniable attraction to her. He hadn't experienced so many feelings in years, and found himself at a loss for what to do with them all. Common sense told him it would be wise to avoid their source, so he'd left the campground early and stayed away the entire day. On a whim, he'd stopped at a book store and picked up a book about communicating with spirits. Maybe he could figure it out on his own. Maybe he didn't need Dove Denning after all.

With nothing else to do and nowhere else to be, he headed back to the campground, hoping for an early dinner and a quiet evening of reading.

Arriving home, he was greeted by the sound of voices in the kitchen. Poking his head in the door, he saw Mick sitting at the table, polishing off the wedding cake. Dove stood at the counter, making a tossed salad. A tantalizing aroma drifted from the oven.

"Hey, dude, you're just in time. We picked up a couple of strombolis for dinner."

His glance moved again to Dove. It looked like she was settled in for the evening. So much for avoiding her.

"Hey, you'll never guess what movie I picked up for tonight," Mick said, moving to the oven.

"Friday the Thirteenth."

"Close." He opened the oven door and pulled out a cookie sheet containing two overstuffed strombolis. "Nightmare on Elm Street. I invited Ms. Denning to stay and watch it with us. I hope that's okay."

He forced a smile. "It's fine." Thank you, Mick.

They sat down at the table, Dove sliding into the chair opposite him. Dusty had never been more aware of himself, had never felt more awkward or tongue tied. Thankfully Mick kept up a steady stream of chatter, sparing him having to make conversation.

With the meal finished, they stacked the plates in the sink and moved into the living room. Mick removed the DVD from its case and popped it into the player, then settled himself in the chair, leaving Dusty no choice but to join Dove on the sofa. He did his best to concentrate on the movie, but couldn't seem to keep his eyes from returning to her again and again. He liked the way her hair curled on her shoulders, and the soft curve of her cheek. Her nearness and the sweet scent of her perfume called to mind his recent dream, and for a moment he allowed himself to imagine how heavenly it would be to take her in his arms and continue the kiss. But daydreams like that were neither wise nor productive, and so he steered his thoughts back to movie.

Stealing another glance at Dove's face, it became clear to him that she'd accepted the invitation more to avoid hurting Mick's feelings than for any desire to view blood and guts. When it was finally over, she stood. "That was an interesting movie, Mick. Thanks for inviting me to watch it."

"This was only the first part. We could rent part two tomorrow, if you wanted."

"Let's see how much homework you've got tomorrow before we make too many plans," Dusty said. Dove's grateful glance was not lost on him. Following her to the kitchen, he grabbed his coat from the back of a chair. "I'll go with you. It's bound to be a spooky walk back down the path."

The trail was dark and strewn with shadows, and she instinctively reached for his hand as they walked. "He sure loves those horror movies, doesn't he?"

"He can't get enough of them. Rents them every year at this time, a different one every night."

"Poor you."

"I take it you didn't enjoy it?"

"I hated it."

He laughed. "I suspected as much."

They walked the rest of the way in quiet, Dusty savoring the warmth and softness of her hand nestled in his. When they reached the cottage, she unlocked the door and he followed her inside. The cottage was unpleasantly cool. Across the room, the curtains fluttered in the open window.

"You'll want to remember to remember to close your windows when you go out. The days can be warm, but the nights get pretty nippy out here this time of year."

"I don't remember opening it." A bewildered expression crossed her face. "But I guess I must have."

"You don't think it was the boogeyman, do you?"

"That's not funny." She crossed the room and slid the window shut.

"Do you want me to light a fire for you? Take the chill off?"

"That would be wonderful."

He felt her eyes on him as he knelt and arranged a pile of kindling in the grate. Selecting a log from the pile, he placed it on top and lit a flame. Moments later a fire roared to life, bathing her hair and skin in its soft glow. For a moment he ached to take her in his arms, to hold her beauty close to his heart. But that was just another useless daydream.

"This is nice, Dusty," she said. "Can you stay and enjoy it with me for awhile?"

He would have liked to. Would have loved to. But he didn't trust himself. Not tonight, not feeling the way he did. "I should head back and make sure Mick's doing his homework."

"All right."

She seemed disappointed, but maybe it was his imagination. He didn't know enough about women to say. He didn't seem to know anything anymore. "Would tomorrow be a good day to drive out to Crystal Mountain?" he blurted. "We could look at the leaves."

She smiled. "Tomorrow would be a perfect day."

"Great. Pick you up at ten?"

"I'll look forward to it."

Walking back, he paused to catch his breath. Somewhere between dinner and the movie's end he'd decided that ignoring her would not serve any purpose. She had things he needed, things he couldn't get anywhere else. She'd lied to him, and in Dusty's experience, people lied for one of two reasons. Either they were afraid of something, or they had something to hide. Either way, it was up to him to earn her trust. As they said, slow and steady won the race and so he'd proceed, slowly and with caution.

•

As silly as it had been, the movie unsettled her. When Dusty left, Dove poured a glass of wine and carried it back to the fireplace. She'd just settled into a chair when her cell rang. Tchaikovsky. She smiled.

"Hello, Mark."

"Thought I'd check in. How are things?"

"Fine. How's life in the big city?"

"Same as ever. Erin and I stopped by your place tonight. She watered your plants while I went through your mail."

"Anything interesting?"

"Luckily, no."

"It's been two weeks."

"Two weeks today."

"It was probably just some jerk, right?"

"The world is full of them, babe. Still, I'm glad you're tucked away up there for awhile. The guy's definitely not playing with a full deck and I don't like the implications in that letter. "

"Some sort of religious fanatic."

"They can be the worst ones."

"Well, Sewall had a change of heart," she said, sipping her wine. "Maybe this guy did, too."

"Yeah, maybe. But until we know for sure I still want you to be extra careful."

"I will."

"So, are you going stir crazy yet?"

"Actually, no. Tonight I watched my first-ever horror flick, and tomorrow I have a date to go leaf-peeping."

He laughed softly. "Sounds like you're broadening your horizons."

After receiving an update on his daughter, Izzy, she disconnected the call and moved to the window. Gazing out at the darkness, she tried not to think about the letter, but found it was engraved on her mind. Seventy-four words made up of mismatched letters cut from magazine ads that had squeezed her already over-stressed nerves to the breaking point.

> *Be not deceived! Evil will be hunted down and destroyed wherever it is found. There shall not be among you any that use divination, nor any enchanters, nor those who consult with spirits, nor any WITCHES. For those who do these things are an abomination unto the Lord: and He shall drive them out from before you. The land shall be purged of wickedness. The accursed shall be purified by fire.*
> —Samuel Sewall

The Sarah Waterman case had horrified the city, and Dove's role in it had been publicized more than she would have liked. For weeks after the trial the letters and emails and phone calls from strangers had been almost constant. Most of them commend her for her talent and courage. But publicity also attracted weirdos. She'd received a dozen marriage proposals, and just as many letters reproaching her for her interference in the case. Most disturbing was the Samuel Sewall letter. She'd looked up the scripture, a verse from the Old Testament book of Deuteronomy that in his frenzied state the writer had added to and twisted into a threat. She would have written it off as just another oddball, had a second letter not arrived three days later.

The hunt is on.
—Samuel Sewall

With its arrival, it became obvious to both Dove and to Mark that the man intended to launch a modern day witch hunt. Never mind that she was no more a witch than the nineteen innocent women sentenced to hang by the Massachusetts judge in 1692. Guilt or innocence hadn't mattered then and it wouldn't now. Not to people like this guy.

Shuddering, she locked the window and pulled the drapes closed. In the bedroom, she shrugged out of her parka and hung it in the closet. As she slid the door closed, an expanse of empty space registered in her mind's eye. Opening the door again, she stared in disbelief. Over stimulated by the horror movie, her mind went into fright mode as she flipped through each garment, checked and rechecked the hangers, trying to come up with a suitable explanation all the while knowing there was none. A chill whispered down her spine as she stared at the empty clothes hanger where that morning her cream colored gown had hung.

Chapter Five

The next morning Dove awoke before dawn, feeling energized and eager to see what the day would bring. She'd slept well, all things considered. Sliding out of bed, she padded to the closet, opened the door, and peered inside, as if sheer optimism would make her dress reappear. With no such luck, she closed the door and made her way to the kitchen to start a pot of coffee. As its welcome aroma filled the air, she sat down at the table to wait. Her thoughts returned to the missing gown.

Mick's horror movie had spooked her senseless last night, almost making her believe there was some sort of sinister undercurrent beneath the gown's disappearance. Refreshed by a good night's sleep, she could see now what must have happened. There was only one logical explanation and she would almost rather have attributed it to the boogeyman than to accept the truth.

She thought back to the wedding reception and all of the compliments she'd gotten on the dress. One teenaged girl in particular, Wendy Something, had been particularly taken with the gown, inquiring twice as to where Dove had bought it. Wendy was the same size as Dove, give or take an inch. Certainly small enough to squeeze through the open window. She sighed. In all fairness, it could have been any number of people who'd stolen the dress. A lot of the permanent campers were still at Shadow Lake, getting their trailers buttoned down for winter and enjoying the last, mild days of the season. With no way to prove her suspicions and no desire to raise a fuss, Dove made up her mind to count the dress among her losses and be more careful about the window from now on. With that settled she poured a cup of coffee and carried it to the living room.

Gazing out at the water, a sense of calm came over her. Mornings on Shadow Lake were nothing short of magical. She sucked in a breath as she watched the sun rise in quiet beauty, its colors streaking the sky like a watercolor painting, a blanket of filmy mist enveloping the earth below.

Her eye was drawn to a figure rowing across the lake. Sipping her coffee, she watched as he drew nearer, and was surprised to see that it was Dusty. He looked peaceful, there in the mist, as beautiful and uncomplicated as the painting that stretched out before her and she could only wonder what brought him out at such an early hour. It occurred to her that he was a man of solitude, of secrets. A good man, steady and strong. She watched as he pulled the boat onto the sand, tethered it to the dock, and then walked off into the fog. She smiled. The morning air was chilly, but the brightening sky promised a mild day and she was looking forward to spending it with Dusty.

After a leisurely breakfast, she showered and changed into a pair of black jeans and her favorite oversized cardigan in a shade called ginger spice. At ten o'clock she caught sight of him walking up the path and hurried outside to meet him. Seeing her on the porch, he smiled. "Morning, Dove."

"Good morning."

"Did you sleep all right, or did Mick's silly movie keep you awake 'till all hours?"

"I slept just fine."

"Glad to hear it."

She fell into step beside him as they strolled up the path. The weather was glorious, and she inhaled deeply, enjoying the mingled scents of pine and fresh air and the clean, soap and water scent that clung to him. When they reached the waiting pickup truck, he opened the passenger door for her. "I have an errand to run before we head over to Crystal Mountain, if you don't mind."

"Not at all."

He drove into the city and pulled up in front of a squatty gray building called The A-OK Print Shop. "I left some flyers here to be printed yesterday," he told her. "They said they'd have them ready this morning."

He went inside, returning a few moments later with a large,

rectangular box. Sliding behind the wheel, he opened the lid and pulled out a flyer. Curious, Dove peered at the glossy, nine-by-twelve advertisement featuring whimsical ghosts and comical skeletons. Bold black lettering advertised a "Spooktacular" Halloween party at Shadow Lake Campground.

"This sounds like fun," she said.

"We do it every year. Shane likes to get the town involved in the festivities. That way people can have some fun and we can attract new business at the same time."

"Do you get a big crowd?"

"Pretty fair, usually. It's mostly people from the lake community, but we're branching out this year to try and draw from the city as well. Shane didn't know if we should go ahead with it this year, with he and Emma being out of town, but I told him Mick and I could handle it."

"I'll be glad to help, if there's anything I can do."

He winked. "I might just take you up on that."

"What goes on at this party?" she asked, genuinely interested. It all sounded so down-home and charming.

"The usual. Apple bobbing and a haunted hayride for the kids. A costume parade with prizes. Later on we throw a masquerade party for the grown ups."

"It sounds delightful."

"It is, I guess. We're going to have an awful lot of pumpkins to carve next week. You might be sorry you volunteered to help."

"I'm up for it, but you'll have to tell me what to do. I've never carved a pumpkin before."

He shot her a surprised glance. "You're kidding, right?"

"I wish I was." Even in the best of times, Sophia had forbidden Halloween to be celebrated in her home, substituting instead a no-holds barred costume party for Dove and her friends on the first weekend in November. It was years before Dove understood that the holiday was too painful for her mother, that the ghosts and the goblins were all too real.

After a thirty-minute drive they crossed into Arcadia Township, a cute little village with big red barns and tall white steeples nestled among the foliage. Main Street was lined with rows of enticing little shops. After giving her a short tour, Dusty pulled into a parking lot at the foot of a magnificent mountain. He parked the truck and guided her toward the ski lift. As she stood, looking up, her stomach clenched.

"It sure is a long ways up there, isn't it?"

He regarded her thoughtfully. "Afraid of heights?"

"Maybe just a little."

"We don't have to go up."

"I'm sure I'll be fine once I get up there." She glanced upward again, hoping her nerves would hold up.

They stopped at a pay booth, where Dusty bought two tickets. Taking her by the elbow, he steered her toward the chair lift. She settled in beside him with a nervous smile. There weren't many things in life she was afraid of, but being suspended from a cable hundreds of feet above the earth topped the list. Beads of sweat broke out on her forehead. What had made her think she could do this? *Breathe in*, she told herself. *Breathe out.*

Dusty dropped an arm around her shoulder and squeezed gently. "You okay?"

"I'm fine." Her stomach fluttered as their chair began its creaking ascent up the hillside and she clamped her eyes shut, not at all certain she wouldn't faint.

Sliding his hand in hers, Dusty began to talk, pointing out the scenery their lofty vantage point allowed. The slow, rhythmic sound of his voice had a calming effect. She had no idea why being with this man made her feel safe, but after a few moments she was able to relax and look around. The view above the treetops was spectacular, a fanfare of reds, oranges and golds. It was one of the most gorgeous displays of nature she'd ever seen, and she squeezed his hand, all at once glad he'd invited her to share it with him.

At the top of the mountain the lift abruptly stopped and they got off. They stood for long moments, silently drinking in nature's masterpiece and enjoying each other's company. She was sorry when the moment ended and they climbed back onto the ride.

As their chair bumped along on the overhead cables, their talk turned to the campground and the lake community. "A lot of the families have lived on the lake for generations," Dusty told her. "Everybody knows everybody else, just like in any small town."

"I took a long walk along the lake yesterday. There are some gorgeous homes out there."

"Yes, there are. Especially on the west end. How far did you go?"

"I turned back when I got to an abandoned bait and tackle shop."

His eyebrows lifted in surprise. "Jerry's place? That's halfway around the lake. I guess you did take a long walk."

"I picked up some pretty strong vibes from the place." She hesitated. He'd acted strangely the last time they'd discussed ghosts. She didn't want to bring up the subject again and risk spoiling the day. But her desire to know about the building won out over her good judgment, so she took a chance. "Was there ever a murder there?"

His eyebrows knit together in thought. "At Jerry's? Not that I know of. Not recently, anyway. It's been abandoned for more than twenty years."

"Whatever happened to Jerry?"

"He went out on a toot in his rowboat one morning and is presumed drowned. His dog washed up on the shore a few days later, but the old man's body was never found."

"How sad." She thought of the German shepherd she'd seen pacing on the dock. Reminding herself the day was too pretty to spoil with negativity, she resolutely pushed the image away.

With the ride over and their feet once again safely on the ground, Dusty suggested lunch at a tavern called The Bayberry Inn. Built in the late 1800s, the enormous brick structure had occupied the corners of Bay and Fenderson Streets since the town's founding, according to the sign out front. Inside, the tavern smelled pleasantly of old wood and cinnamon. One entire wall was dominated by a stone fireplace while pierced tin chandeliers hung from the vaulted ceilings. Deep green candles flickered from pewter candlesticks on square pine tables draped in muslin cloths.

A waitress seated them at a cozy table near the hearth. With the enormous fireplace blazing, the room was uncomfortably warm and Dove shrugged out of her sweater. Following suit, Dusty removed his jacket, and her perfect day began to unravel.

His sleeve rode up and she saw his tattoo clearly; a blue bird perched on a branch, intricate cursive letters spelling out a name. Not the name of a long, lost lover, as she'd first thought. The name of a beloved daughter.

Chelsea.

•

He couldn't help but notice her noticing the tattoo. An instant after her eyes moved over it, they flew to her menu. In that instant her entire demeanor changed and she went from being relaxed and candid to anxious and unapproachable. He knew he'd have to be very careful how he played it. Treading carefully, he picked up his menu.

"What looks good?"

"What do you recommend?"

"I've heard they make a mean pot of chili."

"Sold." She closed her menu and glanced around, clearly avoiding eye contact with him. "This is an interesting old building. It looks like they've tried really hard to keep it authentic."

He filled her in on what little history he knew of the town, and by the time the waitress arrived to take their orders she seemed to have regained her composure. They chatted about the Inn, and about some of the fascinating old buildings she'd visited. The exchange was a pleasant give-and-take and Dusty couldn't help congratulating himself on his good fortune. It felt damn nice to be out with a beautiful woman. After feasting on chili, Caesar salads, and thick slices of homemade bread, they splurged on hot apple sundaes.

"I may never eat again," Dove groaned, pushing her half-full dessert plate away.

"Was it worth it, though?"

She grinned. "Every pound I've probably gained."

The waitress returned with the bill. As Dove reached for it, Dusty snapped it up from the table.

"Please let me pay for our lunch, Dusty."

"That's not necessary."

"But you paid for our chair lift tickets. It would only be fair."

"I'm not interested in what's fair. Call me old-fashioned." He winked and dug in his pocket for his thin wad of cash. The day would require all the money he'd allotted himself for the week, but knowing it was the kind of day he would tuck inside his heart to take out and remember when one of his black days came made it worth every dime.

"I'll spring for the tip, then," she said, throwing a ten-dollar bill on the table.

They stepped out of the restaurant and into an afternoon steeped in sunshine.

"This is gorgeous weather for October," she said, glancing up at the cloudless sky.

"It's gorgeous weather for any month. Would you like to take advantage of it and poke around in some of the shops?"

She rewarded him with a smile. "Most men don't like quaint little gift shops."

"I'm not most men."

Chuckling, she tucked her hand under his arm. "Then by all means, let's take advantage."

The main thoroughfare of Arcadia Township consisted of six blocks of picturesque, two-story shops with hand painted signs, old fashioned gas streetlamps and wrought iron benches arranged on hundred-year-old brick sidewalks. Dusty had always thought Arcadia quaint and romantic, a town largely unchanged by time. And though he wasn't exactly an avid shopper, he couldn't think of anywhere he'd rather be than there, with her, on that sun-kissed afternoon.

They spent the next couple of hours browsing in book stores and antique shops, until the temperamental autumn sunshine was swallowed up by clouds, and the heaviness of coming rain hung in the air.

"Maybe we'd better head back," he said.

On their way to the truck, Dove noticed a candle shop tucked into an alley, the brick storefront almost wholly concealed by ivy. Long moments passed as she stared at it, as though unable to tear herself away.

"What an interesting building," she murmured.

"Want to go in?" he asked.

"Yes, I do."

They opened the front door and stepped inside an olfactory wonderland. Scents of every kind reached out and wrapped around them, while new age music swelled softly from hidden speakers. In the rear of the building, a curtain of tinkling bells parted and the owner appeared; an attractive, fifty-something woman with blonde hair and amber colored eyes.

"Welcome," she said.

Dusty nodded and Dove smiled.

"I'm Devon Fairbrother, the proprietor here." With her filmy black dress and beaded choker, Devon Fairbrother was the picture of an eccentric artist. She shook Dusty's hand, and then reached for Dove's, holding it for longer than was necessary. Her eyes locked on Dove's, thoughtful, searching. Something passed between them in the moments before she pulled her hand free, but what it was, Dusty couldn't say.

"I've got a batch of candles in the mold out back that I really must see to. Please, enjoy yourselves." Giving Dove a last, pensive glance, she turned and disappeared through her curtain of bells.

Dusty stared with interest at the items on the shelves as Dove picked up candles and sniffed them delicately, choosing some to purchase and rejecting others. There were aromatherapy lotions and bath crystals, handmade soaps, books on meditation and Yoga. The entire shop was geared toward self-indulgence and Dusty hoped Dove would find something that would soothe her senses. After a half hour of browsing, she settled on a large pumpkin-colored pillar candle and a half dozen votives of various color and scent. Noticing a display of flavored coffees, she selected one called mocha spice and set it on the counter with her candles. She tapped the bell and the candle maker reappeared. Placing the pumpkin-colored candle in a bag, she smiled.

"Mulled Cider. That's one of my very favorites."

"It's heavenly. Do you make all of the candles right here?"

She smiled. "Uh-huh. Candle making is one of my art forms, but my passion is with watercolors. I show some of my work at the gallery next door. The candles are my bread and butter."

"I have to admire anyone who can paint," Dove said. "I've never had that talent."

"There's something I'd like to give you." Reaching under the counter, Devon retrieved two candles and pressed them into Dove's hand. One silver and one black. Though Dusty was surprised by the gift, Dove didn't seem to be.

"Thank you very much."

The candle maker smiled, but her amber eyes were grave. "Take caution," she said.

Strange, Dusty thought. Take caution. Not, Have a nice day, or Come again soon. He sensed a distinct caveat behind the words, but couldn't begin to fathom the reason.

•

By the time they reached Hope Haven it was late afternoon and the rain was coming down in earnest. Dove's mind wandered back over the day, from the amazing foliage to the scrumptious lunch. She thought of the candle maker and the gifts she'd given her. An indigo candle, invoking inertia. And a silver one, to remove negativity.

She'd been drawn to the old building at first glance, felt compelled to go inside, as if pulled by centrifugal force. She'd known from the moment their skin made contact that Devon Fairbrother was a kindred spirit. One of the gifted. Feeling a chill that had little to do with the damp weather, she pulled her sweater closer around her and wondered what the candle maker had seen in her eyes.

"I was going to drop off some flyers in town," Dusty said, breaking into her thoughts. "But maybe that would be better saved for another day."

As they climbed the winding road that led to the campground, they talked about the upcoming Halloween party. Dove was lulled by the soft thumping of the windshield wipers and the pleasing rhythm of Dusty's voice. All in all it had been one of the nicest days she could remember.

When they were three or four miles from the campground she noticed an elderly woman walking in the distance. She hobbled along the graveled road, as if every step was agony. Dove glanced at Dusty for his reaction. Seeing none, she turned her gaze back to the woman. The poor thing didn't even have an umbrella. She chewed her lip, hoping Dusty would offer her a ride. As the truck drew closer, the woman turned. A smart black cap covered her silver curls, its netted veil partially concealing the woman's face. Her eyes locked on Dove's an instant before she stepped in front of the truck.

"Watch out!" she screamed.

Impressions enveloped her like mist as she passed through the woman's essence; gnarled fingers hanging wash out on a clothesline, and again, gliding effortlessly over a keyboard. Gentle fingers stroking the talcum powder softness of a baby's skin, a loving voice singing a lullaby. They lingered for but a moment, and then disappeared.

Dusty swerved to the shoulder of the road, braking hard. "What happened?"

She was trembling, unable to catch her breath. "I'm sorry."

"What did you see?"

"Nothing. I'm so sorry."

"It's alright." He put a hand on her hair, stroked gently. "It's alright."

But it wasn't alright. His eyes mirrored all the alarm, all of the unmitigated concern of eyes that looked upon a madwoman. God help her, maybe she finally had gone mad. For the first time in her life, she hadn't been able to distinguish the dead from the living. A sob escaped her, and he pulled her into his arms. He held her for a long moment as rain pounded on the roof.

"Alright now?" he asked.

"Yes. I'm so sorry. I don't know what came over me."

"It's all right, Dove. I often think I see things darting out into road. Especially in a heavy rain."

She was grateful for his tact. As they continued their slow journey along the road, Dusty kept up a steady stream of conversation. But he talked too fast, too cheerfully, and she knew it was an attempt at covering up his embarrassment and the truth she'd seen radiating from his eyes. The one that plainly said he felt sorry for her. She turned her face to the window, tuning out his words as thoughts of Sophia crept over her, like rain clouds creeping across the sun.

Her earliest recollections of her mother were of a gentle, child-like soul, of soft hands tucking her into bed at night, and an angel-voice singing her and her brother, Christopher, to sleep.

As she and Christopher grew older, there were happy periods of picnics and puppet shows followed by bursts of dementia in which Sophia locked herself in her room for days. During those times there were no bedtime songs, only sorrowful wailing in the night. Dove hid beneath her blankets, hands pressed against her ears to try and block out a horror she hadn't understood at the time, but had grown to know all too well.

Grandmother Christiano always said that if Dove's father had lived, Sophia might have been alright. A big, loud, loving man, Kenneth was like a guard dog, chasing away the ghosts and visions that haunted his fragile wife. When he died unexpectedly at age thirty, Sophia crumbled beneath the pressure of her gifts, under the sheer weight of an obligation she was either too weak or too compassionate to refuse.

With every year that passed, Sophia's grip on reality became more tenuous, her relationship with her children more abusive. In the middle of the night, on his seventeenth birthday, Christopher packed his belongings into a duffel bag and drove off in Sophia's car. The car was eventually found at a Baltimore bus depot. Christopher was never seen again, and thirteen-year-old Dove was left alone with Sophia's madness. A madness she would live in fear of for the rest of her life.

•

Dusty pulled into the campground parking lot to discover his parking space occupied by a late-nineties Chevy. The car was cherry red, with a spider web crack spreading across the windshield. Assorted dents and dings, as well as the mammoth stereo system that occupied most of the back seat identified the vehicle as a teenager's ride. "Looks like Mick's got company," he said.

In the house, he discovered the kitchen filled with smoke and Mick at the stove, frying what was left of a package of hot dogs. An earlier attempt sat in a blackened lump in the sink.

"Hey," Mick greeted them with a grin. "You're just in time for supper."

"Ahh, I think I'll pass."

"Suit yourself. I invited Boots to stay and eat. Is that okay?"

"Just clean up after yourselves when you're done."

Mick's glance swept to Dove. "We stopped and picked up *Nightmare on Elm Street Part Two, Freddy's Revenge*, if you want to watch it with us."

"I don't think I'm up for it tonight, Mick, but thanks anyway."

He shrugged. "Okay."

In the guest room, Dusty shrugged out of his wet clothes and changed into a pair of dry jeans and a sweat shirt. Back in the kitchen, he grabbed up an umbrella.

"Looks like it's starting to let up," he told Dove. "This might be our best shot at a dry walk."

As they headed down the path together, he felt his body stir at her nearness. Despite the incident on the way home, he couldn't remember when he'd enjoyed a day more. He couldn't help wishing it didn't have to end.

When they were safely in her cottage, Dove smiled at him and shook out the umbrella. "Make yourself comfortable while I go and change."

He lit a fire in the fireplace and sat down on the couch to wait for her. Moments later she returned, dressed in a white velour robe. She'd set her hair free of its braid, and it tumbled in loose waves down her back. He caught his breath, wondering how it was possible for a woman to look so good.

"Are you hungry?" she asked. "I'll make sandwiches."

"Thanks, but I'm still full from lunch."

"Me, too. I could use a drink, though. I've got a fresh bottle of wine. Interested?"

He hesitated, considered making an excuse, but in the end, decided to come clean. "I'm an alcoholic, Dove."

Her face colored in embarrassment. "I'm sorry."

"It's all right."

"I had no idea."

"It's all right. Really."

"How about coffee?"

"Coffee would be perfect."

She grabbed the packet of flavored coffee from her shopping bag. He put another log on the fire and prodded the flames to life while Dove got busy in the kitchen. Settling back on the sofa, he opened the bag she'd gotten at the candle maker's shop, pulled out one of the candles and studied it. It was dark blue, speckled throughout with flecks of violet and black. Even unlit, the scent was pungent, a curious mixture of perfume and spice. He'd never smelled anything quite like it before. Curious, he turned it over and read the name on the bottom. "Inertia."

"It stops bad situations from occurring." Dove carried two cups of steaming coffee. Setting them on the table, she took the candle from his hand and lit it.

Bad situations, he thought. Like a sexual encounter with the local drunk?

"At least that's what they say." She lifted both hands and began to knead the base of her neck.

"Your headache's not coming back, is it?"

"I hope not."

He arranged one of the oversized pillows on the floor in front of him. "Come here."

She obediently sat, and he began to massage her neck and shoulders.

"Mmm," she murmured. "That's incredible." After a long moment, she said, "Thank you for today, Dusty. I really had a marvelous time."

"So did I."

"I'm sorry about, you know. Earlier. Screaming like that. If you could have seen your face." A chuckle escaped her lips, and quickly died.

He traced his fingers gently along her spine. "What did you see, Dove?"

He thought she'd avoid the question, and was surprised when she said, simply, "I saw a woman."

He let the word settle in the air for a moment. "A woman?"

"An old black woman in a purple dress. She had on one of those small hats with the netted veils, like women used to wear to church. She was hobbling along the road in a pair of high-heeled shoes, and then ... and then she stepped right out in front of us."

Dusty's hands stopped their work. He stared at her in disbelief. "My God," he whispered. "Patience Wilburt."

She turned. "What?"

"That sounds just like Patience Wilburt. Lord, I haven't thought about her in years."

"Who was she?"

"There used to be a chapel on this road, about four miles down. Patience was the church organist. The Wilburt's didn't own a car. She used to walk from town every afternoon to practice, and every Sunday to play for the services. Morning and evening. I can still remember her walking up the road in those high-heeled shoes. God. That was almost thirty years ago."

"She was struck and killed on this road," she said. "Wasn't she?"

"Yes, she was. I only remember it vaguely. I was still a teenager. But as I recall, the lake community was deeply saddened by it. She was a good woman. A faithful churchgoer. In fact, that afternoon she was on her way to the chapel to watch her great-grandson be baptized. I would have thought a woman like that would rest in peace."

"Sometimes when death comes violently or unexpectedly, or

when something important is left undone, the spirit will retrace its final steps again and again as it tries to come to terms with its loss of physical life. When we," she drew a breath. "When we passed through her, I got the sense of a baby. The desire to witness her grandson's baptism is probably what's holding her here."

Her words were painful. He thought of another life cut short, other dreams left unfulfilled, and he couldn't help but wonder if somewhere, out on Shadow Lake, his daughter was doomed to eternally relive her final moments. The thought was more than he could bear.

"The thing that bothers me most is that I couldn't tell the difference this time." She raised her eyes to his, and he saw they glistened with tears. "I've always been able to tell the difference before."

"You're all right, Dove," he said, stroking her hair. "You're just stressed right now."

"What you asked me the other day ... I wasn't honest with you."

He felt it coming, felt the pressure of it rising within him, like a band tightening around his chest. The confession everything inside him hoped for, and everything inside him resisted.

"I've seen others."

He pulled in a breath, pushed it out. Waited.

"Dusty," she whispered. "Tell me about Chelsea."

Chapter Six

Dusty would think about it later and he'd find it tragically ironic that it happened on his and Colleen's sixteenth wedding anniversary. He'd think it a cruel twist of fate that a day which should have been a logical next step into a well established future would instead mark the beginning of the end.

But he didn't know any of that on that humid July evening as he stood in the bathroom, shaving. Rinsing away the lather, he glanced at the lines thirty-seven years of living had put on his face and he thought about the passing of time. Sixteen years of marriage. Good God, how could time go so fast?

The door opened and Colleen breezed in, wearing a black dress and the string of pearls he'd given her that morning as an anniversary gift. His sidelong glance took in the pleasing lines of her figure. Thanks to her rigorous aerobics program and an admirable amount of willpower, she was still the same slim size eight she'd been on their wedding day. Like everything else in Colleen's well-ordered life, her weight was a project, something to be religiously worked at. His eyes shifted from the mirror and he took a long, hard look at her. The years had been kinder to Colleen than to him. She was attractive, if not beautiful, and he appreciated the care she took with her appearance. And if they weren't madly in love, after sixteen years their marriage was a comfortable habit.

"I went in to say goodbye, but she's still pouting," she told him. Glancing in the mirror, she smoothed a lock of hair. "I bought those little pizzas she likes for dinner but she probably won't eat them out of spite."

His irritation flared at his daughter's selfishness. Colleen had looked forward to the evening for weeks, and would now likely spend it silently seething. He'd not let Chelsea get away with it. Not this time. He splashed on aftershave and walked down the hallway, stopping just short of Chelsea's door. She lay on her bed, face to the window, wearing the same grubby sweat pants and tee shirt she'd worn for the past three days, ever since their blow-up. She looked utterly dejected and his resolve leaked out of him like air from a punctured tire.

"Your mother and I are leaving now, Chelsea," he said. "We'll see you around eleven."

She didn't answer, didn't even acknowledge him. But when he and Colleen were halfway down the staircase, the air reverberated with the thunder of her door slamming shut. A part of him wanted to turn around, march back up the stairs, and throttle her. Another part wanted to try one more time to talk it out, but Colleen was waiting. It was her special evening, and one she richly deserved, so he kept walking, deciding to leave his daughter to her misery.

It was a decision he'd regret for the rest of his life.

"She's become insufferable," Colleen muttered, as he backed their Taurus out of the drive. "Do you think she'll go to the party?"

His hands tightened on the wheel. "She'll be a very sorry little girl if she does."

"Where did we go wrong?"

He sighed. "I don't think we went wrong anywhere, Colleen. She's just being a teenager. They're hard years. For everyone."

"There you go, making excuses for her again. I swear, if I'd acted that way at her age my father would have knocked me into next week."

He knew it was a shot at him and an angry retort formed on his lips. Taking a breath, he decided to let it slide. He'd not argue with Colleen on their wedding anniversary. And he'd not spend the evening brooding over a teenaged temper tantrum, either.

He held Colleen's hand as they walked inside Antoinette's. The hostess immediately seated them at a small, intimate table in the rear, the table he'd requested when he made the reservation two weeks before. With its rich burgundy upholstery, flickering candles, and live piano music, Antoinette's was their favorite restaurant and they'd come every year on their anniversary since they'd married. As soon as they were seated a waitress appeared at their table and he ordered a bottle of Chardonnay, not waiting for Colleen's sanction. Tonight, he would take the reins. Her pleased smile told him he'd chosen well.

They ordered New York Strip steaks and stir fried vegetables and when their meals arrived they dug in with gusto. They chatted amiably about their jobs and their upcoming vacation to Gatlinburg, Tennessee, and Dusty did his best to relax and enjoy the evening. Still, he couldn't keep his mind from wandering back to Chelsea and their earlier altercation. Where had they gone wrong, indeed?

Sensible and determined, Colleen had always believed that there was no problem that couldn't be fixed if only one was willing to work at it. But even steadfast Colleen had been driven to the end of her rope by her daughter's constant rebellion. Headstrong and every bit as determined as her mother, Chelsea made it clear she would not be controlled. Which left Dusty square in the middle.

Colleen had always accused him of being too easy on the girl. In Chelsea's toddler years, Colleen had demanded he put their daughter over his knee, but growing up the way he had, he couldn't bring himself to raise his hand against his child. Had he been too soft with her? He took a swallow of wine and tried to concentrate on what Colleen was saying, but echoes of his unpleasant exchange with Chelsea intruded, casting a bitter shadow over the evening.

If I don't go to the party, then Tyler will go out with someone else.

Then I'd say he's not worth having.

You don't understand!

You're right, Chelse. I don't. Look, I try to be fair. I say yes when I can, but this time I'm saying no.

Why?

They're not a good family. Those boys are always in and out of jail, they drink and they brawl. There's no way I'm letting you go to that party.

This is so unfair!

Sometimes life is unfair.

Life sucks!

Grow up, Chelsea.

Life sucks and so do you and mom. I hate you both...

He sighed, thinking of the sweet child with the sunny smile who'd once adored him. Lord, he missed his little girl.

"You seem like you're a thousand miles away tonight," Colleen commented, watching him closely.

"I'm right here with you," he said, covering her hand with his.

"Right where I belong."

Ironically, he hadn't been sure he was ready, or that he even wanted a child, when Colleen decided it was time. As the months passed, he watched her belly swell with the evidence of new life, both fascinated and terrified of the implications. Months later, he glanced into his baby daughter's eyes and knew he was looking at the greatest accomplishment of his life. He also knew he would never love another human being more.

With the meal finished, he excused himself to go to the men's room. In the lobby, he detoured to the pay phone in the corner. Dropping a quarter into the slot, he dialed home. The answering machine picked up.

"Look, I know you're angry with me, Chels," he said, "But the next time I call, you'd damn well better pick up the phone."

She didn't.

He called from the lobby of the theater when they arrived, and then again halfway through the movie. He'd looked forward to seeing it all week, but now found it impossible to concentrate on the intricacies of the plot. His stomach cramped with worry as his mind chewed on the possible reasons why Chelsea wasn't answering the phone. Spite? Or maybe she had her headphones on, listening to her music at that ear-shattering volume she loved. She certainly wouldn't have disobeyed him and gone to the party ... Would she?

It took every ounce of self control he possessed to sit through the rest of the movie. On the drive home, Colleen wanted to discuss the ending, but she gave up after several unsuccessful attempts to draw him into a conversation.

When they arrived home at a little after eleven, the first thing Dusty noticed was how dark the house looked. The second was a Hope Haven patrol car sitting in the driveway. Squinting through the shadows, he noticed a cop standing on his front porch.

"What on earth do you suppose this is all about?" Colleen asked.

"Hard telling." He pulled in the driveway beside the patrol car.

"I hope she hasn't done anything foolish."

His anger flared. How like Colleen to assume the cop's presence was due to some wrongdoing on Chelsea's part.

The officer turned and walked toward them. "Mr. and Mrs.

Martin?"

"Yes," Dusty said, sliding out of the car. "What can I do for you?"

"Tom Dixon," he said, extending his hand. "How are you folks doing tonight?"

"Fine," Dusty said stiffly.

"Listen, we picked up an eighteen-foot Bayliner on the west side of the lake. I ran the registration and it came back to you."

It was the last thing Dusty expected the cop to say, and he stared at him, dumbfounded, as he tried to process the information. "My boat? Who was driving it?"

"Well that's the strange thing, Mr. Martin. There's nobody in it. It was spotted earlier trawling around the lake. Must have finally run itself out of gas and washed up on the beach. Approximately what time did you folks leave here this evening?"

"Around six." His heart was hammering, his blood roaring in his ears. "Colleen, go inside and see if Chelsea heard any noise out here tonight."

As she hurried toward the house, Dusty turned back to the cop. "You said it was spotted earlier. How long ago was that?"

"Couple three hours. The people didn't report it until just now. Where do you normally keep the boat, Mr. Martin?"

"Dusty?" Both men turned at the scared-sick sound of Colleen's voice. "Chelsea's not here."

Chelsea's not here. Three words that elevated the crisis from a stolen boat to something much, much worse.

The people of the lake community rallied around them. Able-bodied men and women combed the area on foot while the older women made coffee and sandwiches all through the deep, dark night. The next morning the Sheriff's department started dragging the lake. In the early afternoon a special team was called in from Hope County. Dusty watched, feeling strangely detached, as they set up their thermal imaging equipment.

At eight o'clock that evening a human body was detected fifty feet below the lake's surface, tangled in a knot of debris. At eight forty-five he watched as they pulled his daughter's body from the lake. With a glimpse of her pale, beautiful face, his disassociation with the events was shattered. He threw himself on the sand, raging like a madman, tears pouring down his face, one desperate plea hurled at the heavens over and over again. *Chelsea, don't leave us. Baby, please. Don't go.* And in those moments life as he knew it ended. Because she was already gone.

•

When he'd finished speaking, they sat in silence for a long time. Finally, he drew a breath. "She knew better than to go out on the lake without wearing a life jacket. She was an excellent swimmer, won all kinds of trophies for the high school swim team, but still … That lake is nine miles wide and seventy-nine feet deep. Treacherous if you're out there alone at night. Even the best swimmer in the world would get disoriented." His shoulders slumped. "The autopsy showed she was five weeks pregnant. General consensus is she jumped," his voice cracked. "God, I can't make myself believe that."

Dove came to him then, and wrapped her arms around him. His tears were a relief and he let them fall, unashamed, knowing she understood.

"What you can believe is that your daughter loves you very much," she said gently. "She's grieving, just as you are. The night I arrived, I saw her out on the deck. She was very clear in her request. She wanted me to tell you she's sorry."

"What do you think she meant?"

"I'm not sure."

"Do you think you can … get in touch with her?" he added softly, "Right now?"

"I can't make you any promises, Dusty. But I'll try."

He followed as she moved to the sliding door, opened it, and stepped out onto the deck. The evening air held a chill that went straight through his soul.

"Take my hand," she said. He slid his hand in hers, his heart pounding with the fear of not knowing what would come.

Dove turned her face to the sky. She closed her eyes and drew in a breath. Exhaled. Drew another. As if in a trance, she extended her hand, palm out, as if testing the air. "Chelsea," she said, her voice loud and clear. "Your father is here."

He waited for what seemed a quiet eternity. At first he felt nothing but the stillness of the air, heard nothing but his blood slamming through his veins. And then a prickle of electricity raised the hair on the nape of his neck.

"She's here," Dove whispered.

An electrical charge began to hum in the air around him and he braced himself.

"Chelsea!" Dove said.

Gooseflesh raised on his arms, because she spoke with power and authority. Her words were not a request now, but a command, and he waited, heart hammering and eyes anxiously scanning the atmosphere.

"Chelsea, come forth! Your father is here."

Chapter Seven

Dove was a firm believer that destiny made no mistakes and that everything happened for a reason. She felt certain now that the reason she'd come to Shadow Lake was twofold; to help Dusty move on from the tragedy of losing his daughter, and to help Chelsea cross over into a place of peace. It didn't happen last night, but she felt confident it would happen. It was only a matter of time.

Chelsea had been there with them, hovering on the periphery, prevented by fear from making her presence fully known. Dove had felt it in the air, a heartbreaking mixture of longing and trepidation. Underneath it all, Chelsea was just a scared and confused child, and Dove was optimistic that in the end the child's love for her father would win out over her fear. Her thoughts turned to Dusty. So wounded. So full of fear himself. She'd come to care for him more than she wanted to admit, and her desire to ease his pain had made her impatient. She'd rushed the process, scared Chelsea away. Simply put, she'd blown it. She sighed, once again feeling the frustration of having a gift over which she had no control. It had been the same with the ghosts of the Mississippi opera house.

She took a swallow of coffee and turned back to her notes. The opera house had been haunted for more than a century. Six lost souls, each of them desperate for some sort of resolution. No, she thought, make that five souls. That she'd been able to help Johnna Worth was the one bit of gratification that had come out of the whole, messy ordeal. She leafed through a stack of photos until she found the one she was looking for. As she lingered over a black and white shot of Johnna's grave marker shrouded in early morning mist, the whole experience came back to her with disquieting clarity.

She'd traveled all over the world, but had never before experienced the sort of damp, relentless heat that seemed to envelop that small Mississippi town. She'd suffered through it for three days as she built a rapport with the town's residents and plodded through what historical documents she'd been able to glean from the village library. It was slow, painful progress, but on the third day she hit pay dirt. Digging deep into the town's enigmatic roots, she'd discovered that the Warner Hotel and Opera House wasn't all that it seemed. It was much, much more.

Having arrived in town on a Sunday, she'd had to wait until Wednesday for the local Historical Society to open its doors. She'd noticed the weathered, two-story building at the end of Main Street on her first tour of the town. It was plain and unattractive on the outside, but her gut told her she'd find what she needed hidden in its musty corners.

Stepping inside on that humid June morning, she was greeted by the mingled scents of trapped heat and old dust. As her eyes adjusted to the gloom, she saw that the building was long and narrow, the walls on either side flanked by glass cases displaying the town artifacts. Meticulously labeled sepia photographs were arranged neatly on the whitewashed walls above them. In a back corner, an elderly black woman with a close-cropped silver afro and a pair of wire framed glasses sat behind a brand new Dell computer, the only hint of modernization in the room. She glanced up when Dove walked in.

"Good morning," Dove greeted her. "I'm Dove Denning."

The woman nodded. "I know who you are, child. I've been expectin' you." She extended a small, knobby hand. "Sammy Drake."

"It's nice to meet you, Sammy."

"You look warm. Would you like a cold glass of sweet tea?"

Though it was barely nine o'clock, the heat in the building was ferocious. Dove could feel beads of sweat collecting between her shoulder blades. "That would be lovely."

The old woman disappeared into a back room. Dove heard the clink of ice on glass and then Sammy returned with two tumblers of sweet tea. She indicated a small upholstered chair beside the desk. "Won't you please sit down?"

When Dove complied, she handed her one of the sweating

glasses. "I've seen you poking around. What do you think of our little village?"

"It's charming."

"That it is."

Dove sipped the sweet liquid. Cool and soothing as nectar, it was all she could do not to gulp it down. "Have you lived here long, Sammy?"

"All my life."

She went on to explain that she'd taught history at the high school for thirty years, and upon her retirement, became the president of the Historical Society.

"Then you're just the person I want to talk to." Dove pulled out her notebook and pen. "What can you tell me about the town's history, Sammy?"

"I could tell y'all a lot. What is it you want to know?"

"I'm interested in anything you can tell me about the old opera house."

Sammy smiled approvingly, then reached beneath her desk and brought out a box of black and white photos of the Warner Hotel.

"Here it is, child, back when it was brand new. What have you already been told about the building?"

"That it was a magnificent place. A hotel and a restaurant, a place where the town used to gather for parties and dances. They say the opera house was the glue that held the community together."

"It was every bit of that, for certain." She focused her eyes on Dove. "And now I'll tell you something you probably didn't know. The Warner Hotel and Opera House was once a part of the underground railroad."

"You're kidding? I thought the railroad was mostly in the northern states."

"It was. But there was a small group of sympathizer's right here in the Mississippi Delta region. Lowell Warner among them."

Dove settled back in her chair, digesting the information. "Tell me more."

"Lowell Warner moved his family here from Pennsylvania in 1825 and immediately began construction of the Opera House. Of course the town was delighted at the thought of the culture and the jobs the new hotel would bring. With a twenty-room hotel and performances by traveling artists, the opera house would attract rich folks from far and wide. Just what was needed to put this little ol' town on the map. Lowell Warner was showing them just exactly what they wanted to see. " Sammy took a swallow of tea. "What the villagers didn't know was that the hotel had underground passageways, secret rooms down in the cellar. While the wealthy plantation owners were being entertained upstairs, below ground the slaves were making their way to freedom. Lowell Warner was hiding them in plain sight, as they say. Word has it he helped more than fifty men and women find their way to freedom.

"Fascinating."

Once again Sammy fixed her wise old eyes on Dove. "Tell me, child. Have you seen Johnna yet?"

"Johnna?"

"You haven't, then." Sammy looked disappointed.

"Who is Johnna?" Dove pressed.

"Johnna Worth was one of the village girls. Like so many, she came from a large, poor family. At fifteen she got a job working as a maid in the Warner Hotel. Secretly, she was a crusader for the cause. She was a spy, and a damn good one, for who would suspect a shy, pretty girl like Johnna, with her big blue eyes and blonde curls? Johnna became the keeper of the secrets of the cellar."

Dove listened, held captive by the story and the lilting rhythms of the old woman's voice. "Go on."

"After a year or so Johnna fell in love with a slave boy. Her love was the poor girl's undoing in the end. She became pregnant at seventeen, unmarried, of course. If that wasn't disgrace enough, when she gave birth, the child was black. The midwife ran and got the Sheriff. Poor Johnna was shot right there in her in bed."

"Oh, how dreadful."

"They were dreadful times, child." Sammy let her words hang in the air for a moment. "They say that Johnna haunts the opera house. They say she wanders from room to room, searching for her lover. Or at least she did, until recently. Some even claim to have seen her face in the window."

"Have you seen her, Sammy?" Dove asked gently.

"I believe I have, on occasion." She averted her gaze.

Dove's glance wandered to the computer on Sammy's desk and a slow realization dawned. "It was you who sent me the e-mail asking me to come, wasn't it?"

A gentle smile graced the old woman's lips. "Yes, child. It was me."

"Why me?"

"A few years back I attended a seminar at my granddaughter's college in Maryland. You were the guest speaker. Wasn't ten minutes into your presentation before I knew you were the one. I've held on to your card all this time, thinking one day I'd contact you about Johnna. When they tore down the old hotel, well … the time finally seemed right."

"I'm honored," Dove said.

"Do you think you might be able to help her?"

"That's entirely up to Johnna, Sammy. But I want you to know that if she does decide to reveal herself to me, I'll do everything I can to help her find peace."

The phone rang, abruptly ending their conversation. Sammy left her to look at the photos and documents she'd collected for her from the village archives. Dove spent the remainder of the afternoon with her head bent over the dusty volumes. There was precious little to validate Sammy's story about the underground railroad, and Dove wondered if it was a matter of southern pride, or whether the town simply wasn't interested in that fascinating piece of its history. At four o'clock she left the Historical Society and walked three blocks to a diner called The Storybook Café. Four men were seated at a table in the window. As she stepped inside, silence fell over them and she got the uncomfortable feeling she had been the topic of their conversation. She ordered a tuna melt and a bowl of Mississippi chowder, and when her meal arrived she ate ravenously.

She spent the evening in her room at the bed and breakfast, reading a book Sammy had loaned her on the Mississippi River. At ten o'clock, unable to keep her eyes open any longer, she climbed between the cool, linen sheets and fell into a bottomless sleep.

She awakened at midnight with her hands tingling and a sense of urgency clawing at her insides. Pulling on a pair of jeans and a hoodie, she slipped out the front door. The streetlamps glowed softly beneath a pale, yellow moon, lighting her path to the site of the old hotel. Restless energy pulsated in the air around her, and she sat, cross-legged on the ground. Quieting herself, she waited to see who, if anyone, would come forward.

A tingling sensation started in her hands, building to a deep, prickling burn as she concentrated on the barren scrap of land where rubble from the old hotel lay scattered among the ragweed. As she watched, the figure of a woman emerged from out of the shadows, her blonde hair pinned into a bun at her nape. She wore a plain crinoline dress, her feet bare beneath its tattered hem. She was lovely, and Dove sucked in a soft breath.

The woman hovered feet away, her pensive gaze resting on Dove's face. *What have they done with Robert and the others?*

Her aura was magnificent; dazzling white glittering with flecks of red and black. Purity, anxiety and secrecy. Dove sensed no malice within her.

They've taken them away. Do you know where they've taken them to?

Who are you?

As the specter gazed into her eyes, a host of sensations flooded into Dove's awareness; kindness, faithfulness, and love in its purest form.

I'm Johnna.

Dove had learned that sometimes spirits were motivated by a desire for vengeance, driven by the fury of wrongs they'd suffered. In this gentle spirit, she sensed nothing more than a need to tell her story, a yearning to be relived of the burden she'd carried for more than one hundred and fifty years. She pulled in another breath, slowly released it.

They were wrong, Johnna. What they did to you … it was so very wrong.

What have they done with Robert?

The slaves have been freed. All of them. Your work here is done.

She wailed softly.

Johnna, Dove said firmly. *Look at me!*

With extreme concentration, Dove summoned into her conscious mind all of the awareness of history she could gather, channeling into Johnna's spirit the truth of Abraham Lincoln's Emancipation Proclamation, Dr. Martin Luther King, Junior's "I Have A Dream" speech. As each truth was revealed, she felt Johnna's spirit gazing more deeply into her soul.

It's over, Johnna. The battle has been won.

Are you certain of this?

You've been away for a very long time. Society as you knew it has changed tremendously. Blacks are free to live as they please now. She summoned an image of the inauguration of Barack Obama. *The president of the United States is a black man.*

Surely these things can't be?

It's true. All of it. Your child is waiting. Robert is waiting. It's time to lay down your burden and go to them. Your work on earth is done.

Johnna hovered, uncertain. Dove reached out her arms. Weeping, she fell into them. Dove held her, whispering words of encouragement until at last, she felt her slip away into the atmosphere.

Alone again, Dove hugged her knees close to her chest as tremor after tremor shook her body. She sat, breathing deeply, utterly spent, startled when a voice behind her spoke.

"That was quite a show."

She turned abruptly. A man of about her age stood in the shadows, watching her, his face contorted in anger. "I don't know where you come from, Lady, but we don't go in for this sort of thing 'round here."

"What sort of thing?" she asked, standing shakily to her feet.

"Ghosts and goblins." He smiled, but his eyes remained cold. "If there are any spirits lingering here, we believe them to be demonic in nature. I'd prefer it if you'd let me deal with them. My way."

"And who are you?"

"I'm Wesley Wallace, the pastor of the United Church of the Cross. I like to think of myself as this town's spiritual leader."

"These are not demons you've got here, Mister Wallace. They're restless souls. Hurting souls."

"Not to my way of thinking." His smile slipped and his expression grew stony. "Ever since you showed up here I have young girls holding séances and playing with Ouija boards. I'm afraid you've given them some very unhealthy ideas. I think it would be the best thing for all concerned if you'd head on back to where you came from."

A simple request, but she sensed a definite threat beneath his words. She tilted her chin in defiance. "Thank you for your concern, Mister Wallace. I'll leave when my work is done, and not a moment before." Pushing past him, she strode back to the bed and breakfast.

The next morning she was still seething. In her line of work she ran into plenty of resistance. She was no stranger to opposition, but the sheer arrogance of this man brought out her stubborn streak. She'd stay, she decided, until every last spirit had been dealt with. Her way.

•

The Storybook Café was much busier that morning than it had been the previous afternoon. Stepping inside, Dove once again felt a hush settle over the room. She stood by the counter, waiting to be seated while waitresses in stained aprons and scuffed white shoes hustled past, pointedly ignoring her. After several minutes, a young couple with two small children exited their booth by the window and Dove slid into it. After a lengthy delay, a waitress stalked over and slapped a menu on the table.

"I don't need a menu," Dove said. "I'd like a cup of coffee and a cheese Danish, please."

"Soon's I can get to it," the woman mumbled. She scurried away and what seemed an impossibly long time later, returned with a pot of coffee and a cold Danish. She set the plate in front of Dove, sloshed some coffee into her cup, and hurried away again.

The bell above the front door chimed and the silence in the room deepened. Dove glanced up to see a man of around thirty-five standing in the doorway. He had sandy blonde hair and a weight lifter's build. He also had a badge. He strolled over to her table and slid into the seat across from her. "Dove Denning?"

"That's me," she said, taking a swallow of coffee. "What can I do for you, Sheriff?"

"We got a report that someone matching your description was trespassing on the property near the old hotel last night."

She stared at him, incredulous. "I wasn't trespassing. I was merely sitting."

"The property you were sitting on belongs to the Church of the Cross." His gaze dropped from hers as if he was embarrassed. "The church board has asked that we place you under arrest."

She felt her blood pressure climb. "You've got to be kidding."

He removed a grainy photo from his pocket and gingerly set it on the table in front of her. Glancing at it, she saw it was a picture of herself, sitting on the ground beneath a tree, by all appearances, hugging no one. She winced.

"I'm sure you're very good at what you do, Ms. Denning," he said. "But the fact is, you're stepping on some influential toes here. You'd be doing yourself a favor if you left, quietly and without a fuss."

Arching an eyebrow, she gave him a wry smile. "You're running me out of town, Sheriff?"

"Not by choice, believe me." He grinned, and the warmth spread to his large brown eyes. It crossed her mind that under different circumstances she would have found him attractive. Dove Denning was not a woman who scared easily, but this was starting to feel like way more trouble than she needed.

"I'll thank you in advance for your cooperation." He stood and walked from the diner. When he passed by the window, Dove stood and threw a five-dollar bill on the table. Gathering her pride, she breezed from the restaurant, leaving her coffee unfinished.

Back at the bed and breakfast, she put in a call to Sammy at the Historical Society. When the answering machine picked up, she canceled their lunch date for that afternoon, promising to call later that night and fill her in on her encounter with Johnna. Disconnecting the call, she packed her clothes and her notes into her suitcase. She stopped in the office and paid her bill, then got in her car and headed back to Philly, reluctantly leaving the ghosts of the opera house in Wesley Wallace's incapable hands.

Chapter Eight

Dusty knew better than to eat hard candy. His teeth hadn't been in terrific shape when he was a young man, and at his last dental appointment, LaDonna, the young, pretty hygienist had cheerfully informed him that for middle aged men, it was all about maintenance. Middle aged. The words rankled. Hell, at forty-five, classifying him as middle aged was generous, he knew that. Still, having it pointed out always felt like a kick in the teeth.

Be that as it may, LaDonna's advice was valid, and normally he resisted the butterscotch drops and the root beer barrels Emma left sitting around the house in her pretty glass dishes. But on Wednesday morning, engrossed in his new book, he found himself reaching for them without thinking.

He'd have been all right if he'd stopped after the first two. Biting down on the third root beer barrel he heard a sickening crunch. An instant later a ferocious pain shot straight through to his gum. He tried to ignore it, but by early afternoon the pain was excruciating. He called his dentist, who graciously agreed to fit him in at four thirty. He glanced at his watch. One more hour to go.

Hearing a shriek of laughter, he glanced into the living room where Mick and his friend, Wendy, were engaged in a tickle war.

"You can't do that!"

"Yes, I can."

"Dude, you can't just come up and sucker punch my guy. Look, you just lost, like, a bazillion points."

"I won the round, though."

"Dude, you cheated."

"But I won. That's all that matters."

He sighed. Normally he enjoyed having Mick's friends around, enjoyed the happy chaos that only teenagers could create. Today the noise set him on edge. He popped a couple of aspirins in his mouth and chased them with a glass of water, being careful to avoid the tender area in his lower left gum.

The fact that Mick's guest of the day was female left him with another problem. It wasn't that he didn't trust Mick, but the boy was at an age where innocent situations could easily get out of hand. He'd be gone at least a couple of hours. What would Shane want him to do?

He was staring out the window, mulling over his dilemma when he caught sight of Dove walking up the path. She looked half her age in a pair of faded jeans and an oversized sweatshirt, her hair cascading to the middle of her back. A familiar heat pooled in his lower regions. Middle aged or no, whenever he was in Dove's presence he felt like a boy. He'd been drawn to her at first glance and his attraction had grown with every moment they spent together. The intimacy of the experience they'd shared the night before, trying to connect with Chelsea, had thrown his feelings into overdrive. He'd never been quixotic over a woman before. What he'd felt for Colleen hadn't even come close. Watching Dove walk toward him, he wondered if it was possible he was falling in love.

After a soft knock, the door opened and she stepped into the kitchen, bringing with her the exotic perfume of her night sky candles. She smiled. "I thought I'd stop by and see how you're doing today."

"I'm fine. At least I was until I had a close encounter with a root beer barrel."

Her eyes skimmed his face. "What did you do, crack a tooth?"

"Sure feels that way."

"Oh, no."

"It's my own darn fault." He indicated the dish of root beer barrels. "Emma's addicted to these things. I should know enough to leave them alone." His glance was drawn to the window again when a blue pickup truck pulled into the lot.

"Who's that?" Dove asked.

"Polly Church. She lives across the lake."

"I wonder what she wants."

"I've got a pretty good idea."

He watched as the older woman climbed out of the truck and slowly approached the house. Polly was sixty-five if she was a day, but Dusty had always thought of her as being much younger. Polly'd married as a teenager. She'd had a rough go of it in life, living with Benny Church all those years. After his death, she was like a beautiful butterfly suddenly released from a jar. She'd gone back to college and earned a degree in horticulture and in the years since, led a busy, active life as a public speaker and crusader for wildlife. The folks around the lake agreed it was Polly's passions in life that kept her young.

As she drew near, he noticed the slowness of her gait and the tired lines that were etched into her face and couldn't help wondering if she was unwell. He opened the door as she climbed onto the porch.

"Hello, Polly. What brings you to our side of the lake?"

"Sorry to bother you, Dusty." She grasped the hand rail, obviously winded. "Wendy didn't get off the school bus this afternoon and I was hoping Mick might know where she is. They tell me she's been cutting her classes. I don't really know if she was in school today at all. She doesn't answer her cell phone."

"Actually, Wendy's here. I assumed you knew."

Some of the tension left the old woman's face. "Thank the good Lord for that." Her gaze rested for a moment on Dove. "I'm Polly Church. I don't believe we've met."

"Dove Denning," Dove extended her hand. "I'm an old friend of Emma's."

"Glad to meet you."

"Mick, come on out here a minute," Dusty hollered.

Within moments Mick appeared in the kitchen, his dark shadow of a girlfriend following.

"Aunt Polly," she said, clearly less than pleased to see the old woman. "Did you come here to check up on me?"

"I didn't know where you were and I was worried." A slight edge crept into Polly's voice. "I don't think checking up is unreasonable, under the circumstances."

"I'm fine. I'm right here."

"I can see that, now. Why didn't you call me?"

"I thought you'd be resting. I didn't want to bother you."

Polly's glance slipped away. She was old school and Dusty knew it embarrassed her to air her dirty laundry in front of them. "We'll talk about this later."

"I'm sorry, Mrs. Church," Mick said. "I invited Wendy to come over and play video games. I didn't mean to worry you."

"It's not your fault, Mick." Her gaze once again rested on her niece. "I'd like you home in an hour."

"Aunt Polly!" the girl wailed.

"I don't want you walking along the lake road after dark. I've told you that."

"But Mick invited me to stay for supper. We're going to watch a movie later."

To Dusty's surprise, Dove broke in, "I'd be happy to give her a ride home later, Polly, if you're comfortable with that."

"I'd hate to put you out."

"It's no bother, really."

"Sweet," Mick said. He and Wendy banged their knuckles together in some sort of teenaged code.

"No later than seven thirty," Polly said sternly.

"Eight o'clock."

"Seven thirty and that's the end of it, Wendy. You have a history project due next week. We're going to sit down and get at it tonight."

Wendy blew out a breath. "All right."

As the two teens headed back to the living room, a sad smile crossed Polly's face. "I know I must seem terribly inept at all this."

"You're doing the best you can, Polly," Dusty said. "That's all anyone can ask."

"That's what I keep telling myself." Her gaze wandered across the parking lot and returned. "When are Shane and Emma due back?"

"First of the month," Dusty told her.

"Such a lovely couple."

"That they are."

They chatted for a moment more, and then Polly turned to leave. "I've still got a load of wash on the line, so I'll say goodbye now. Thanks again. Both of you." As she got into her truck and drove away, Dove gave him a questioning glance.

"I'll fill you in later," he said, lowering his voice though Mick had restored the volume on his game system to somewhere between loud and ear-piercing. "Right now I've got to head out myself. My dentist has agreed to squeeze me in this afternoon."

"Good luck."

"Thanks." He unconsciously rubbed his jaw. "Listen, Dove, would you mind hanging out here for a little while?" He gestured toward the living room, dropping his voice again. "I don't know quite what their situation is. I mean, they seem to be just friends, but Mick's at an age ... I'd hate to see them get into trouble."

She arched an eyebrow. "You want me to chaperone them?"

"If you wouldn't mind. I shouldn't be more than a couple of hours."

"All right." She grinned. "But you'll owe me."

"How about dinner?"

"That would be a start."

Her playful tone wasn't lost on him and he felt his face grow warm. Was she flirting with him?

"I thawed a package of hamburger. Seeing we're going to have a dinner guest, maybe you can help me figure out something interesting to do with it."

A smile played at her lips. "Go and see about that tooth. I'll take care of everything."

He smiled. Damn, it was nice having a woman around.

Driving toward the city, his thoughts returned to Polly Church. She was going to have her hands full with Wendy, of that he was certain. From there his thoughts bridged to Chelsea and he felt a familiar stab of pain, a pain that hadn't eased for one moment of one day in the last eight years. Polly needn't have apologized for her ineptness. When it came to raising a teenaged girl he was the picture of incompetence. He wanted so badly to talk to his daughter one more time, to understand what happened that night. To say goodbye. He'd failed miserably last night.

According to the book he'd bought on supernatural phenomena, negative thoughts interfered with spirit energy, discouraging visitations. He vowed that next time he'd keep himself calm. He'd fill his mind with positive, loving thoughts. Next time he'd do it right.

He sighed. If there was a next time.

He'd never put any stock in things like séances and crystal balls, but he had to admit, the book made sense. If spirits existed, then he supposed there were people who could communicate with them on some visceral level. Just because he didn't happen to be one of them didn't make it any less possible.

He'd only intended to read the chapters on ghosts, but finding himself engrossed, he'd read the book from cover to cover. He thought about the unit he'd read on psychics, how they sometimes saw not only the ghosts of the past, but of the future as well, and he felt a twinge of sadness for Dove. He couldn't imagine what it must be like to try and live in two worlds. It was no wonder her mother had gone mad.

The nagging feeling he'd had while reading returned. Something she'd said, something that now eluded him, left him with a troubled, uneasy feeling deep in his gut. As he ground his teeth together, trying to remember, a blazing pain shot through his gum, scattering his thoughts of the supernatural.

•

Dove did her best to keep up with the video game, which seemed to consist of car chases, fist fights, and blaring rap music. After awhile she gave up and watched the kids instead. Wendy fascinated her, with her black clothes, black eyeliner, and a sprinkling of blonde roots at the scalp of her inky black hair. The Goth look was fading in popularity at the university, but it seemed to be alive and well in the halls of American high schools. She couldn't help wondering why kids were so preoccupied with death these days. For some the look was merely a passing fad, like Mick's mohawk and lip ring, but she sensed darkness in Wendy. An uncomfortably genuine bleakness dimmed her aura, speaking of a great unhappiness within the girl.

When the game was over at last, she stood.

"You're not leaving now, are you?" Mick asked. "Friday the Thirteenth is coming on Cinemax in fifteen minutes."

"I think I'd better wander out to the kitchen and see what I can find for dinner," she said, grateful for the excuse.

She considered the package of hamburger Dusty left thawing on the counter, and hoped she could make good on her promise. Searching through the cupboards, she saw that Emma's kitchen was well stocked with spices. Her first thought was a pan of Hungarian goulash, but not finding any pasta, she grabbed a five-pound bag of potatoes from the pantry and quickly adjusted her plan. She selected ten good sized potatoes and was rinsing them in the sink when Wendy wandered out to the kitchen.

"Need any help?"

Dove smiled. "Don't you want to watch the movie?"

"I've already seen it a million times."

"You can help me peel some of these potatoes, if you'd like."

She set Wendy up at the sink with the potatoes and a paring knife and moved to the stove, where she began to brown the ground beef.

"What are you making, anyway?" Wendy asked.

"Shepherd's Pie."

"Is it any good?"

"I think so. Never had it?"

"My mom doesn't like to cook. We mostly eat microwave dinners or fast food." She slashed her knife across a potato. "Can you believe Aunt Polly actually bakes her own bread every Wednesday? And pies, too." Her brow wrinkled. "She's hopelessly old-fashioned."

"You say that like it's a bad thing."

"It's just ... weird, that's all. Like her coming here looking for me today. That was embarrassing."

"She was worried about you."

"She doesn't have to worry about me. I can take care of myself. My own mother never cares where I am half the time, why should Aunt Polly?"

Dove searched her mind for a word of wisdom and came up empty. She was forty years old and childless. What did she know about any of it? She had no idea what circumstances had led to Wendy's being taken in by the old woman, but she was betting they weren't pretty.

"I can imagine it's a big adjustment for both of you," she finally said.

"It is." Wendy looked as though she wanted to say more, but in the end she merely shrugged.

Dove boiled the potatoes, mixed in the beef and the spices, and sprinkled Parmesan cheese over the top of her creation before sliding it into the oven. She'd just finished preparing a tossed salad when Dusty returned. He smiled at her, warming her from the inside out.

"How's your tooth?" she asked.

"Good as new."

"Ready for dinner?"

"I thought you'd never ask."

She and Wendy set the table and they all sat down to eat. Dusty and Mick heaped their plates, while Wendy took a tentative spoonful. As Dusty sampled her creation, Dove watched closely for his reaction.

"How'd I do?"

"Excellent," he said, around a forkful of potatoes. "This is a lot better than the sloppy Joe's I was planning to make."

"It's freakin' amazing, Ms. Denning," Mick said, shoveling in another forkful. "You should seriously give Miss Emma the recipe."

Wendy conceded that the meal was "not bad," though Dove noticed she helped herself to seconds. After a lively debate over who was creepier, Freddie Kruger or Jason, Mick and Wendy's talk turned to school and the upcoming art show.

"You should seriously enter it, Wend," Mick said.

"Nah."

"If I could draw like you, I would. First prize is a hundred bucks."

"Like I'd win, anyway," she said, rolling her eyes.

"You would. Your pen and ink was the best one in class. Probably in the whole school."

"Oh, shut up!" But Dove saw a flush of pink color Wendy's cheeks and knew Mick's praise pleased her.

With the meal finished, she and Dusty cleaned up the kitchen while the teens headed back to the living room.

"Join me for a cup of coffee?" Dusty asked.

She glanced at the clock. "I'd like to, but it's after seven. I should probably run Wendy home."

"I'll take her, if you'd rather not."

She smiled. "I don't mind."

"Stop in when you get back and I'll walk you home."

"Great. Maybe we can have that cup of coffee at my place."

Throwing caution to the winds, she put the invitation out there, but if he caught the subtle message she'd hoped to convey, he didn't show it. Driving down the lake road, she wondered whether she'd made a mistake. She was attracted to him like she hadn't been to any man in years, but was she rushing things?

"Can I ask you something, Ms. Denning?" Wendy said, breaking in on her thoughts.

"Uh-huh."

"Has Mick ever said anything about me?"

Sensing land mines beneath the question, she chose her words with care. "Not that I recall. But I really don't talk with Mick that often. Why?"

"I don't know." She shrugged. "I just get a vibe from him sometimes."

"What kind of vibe?"

"Like the kind that's there when Dusty looks at you."

The words caused a jolt, but she kept her tone casual. "What do you mean?"

"Like he's mad in love or something."

As Dove digested the words, Wendy said, "He asked me to help decorate for the Halloween party next week."

"Who did?"

"Mick," she said, exasperated.

She was distracted, flabbergasted by Wendy's observation. *Get yourself together*, Dove. "That sounds like fun."

Wendy shrugged. "I'll help decorate, but I'm not going to the party."

"Why not?"

"I don't have a costume."

"What do you want to be?"

"I'd like to dress up as a fortune teller. I was thinking I could do palm readings for the kids at the party. But I can't wear just anything, and the costumes you get around here are so lame." She studied her fingernails. "There's a sweet costume shop in West Union, where I used to live, but Aunt Polly is afraid to drive that far."

It was clearly a hint, and thinking it over, Dove decided to take the bait. "I don't have a costume either. Maybe we could go to West Union together."

"Do you mean it?"

"I wouldn't have said so if I didn't. When would you like to go?"

"Well, my school's closed on Friday for teacher conferences. We could go then, if you want to."

"Let's plan on it."

She navigated through a labyrinth of narrow roads until Wendy directed her down a street called Whispering Sands Lane. "This is it. Last house on the right."

Within moments she pulled up in front of a pretty, blue-shingled house with cheerful red shutters. The porch lamp glowed, bathing the yard in a pool of light. Dove took note of the gardens, where mums and late-blooming flowers clustered around fountains and rock walls. Birdhouses of every shape and size peeked from the branches of at least a dozen fruit trees.

"Look at all the birdhouses."

"Aunt Polly makes them."

"Really?"

"They're part of her nest box project," she said, opening the door. Dove would have liked to question her further, but the girl was clearly agitated. "There she is in the window. Thanks for the ride."

"No problem."

She hesitated. "You won't forget about Friday, will you?"

"No, Wendy. I won't forget."

"Cool." Dove watched as she slid out of the car and disappeared inside the house.

•

If he didn't know better, Dusty might have thought Dove was interested in him. But what seemed like a crystal clear signal was surely his imagination. It had to be, because no way in hell would a woman like Dove Denning want anything from him. With that thought firmly in his head, he went outside to meet her. "How was your trip?"

"Uneventful. Are you ready for that coffee now?"

His stomach constricted. Reminding himself it was an invitation for coffee and nothing more, he took her elbow and guided her down the path.

After a few quiet moments passed, she said, "Tell me about Wendy."

"I don't really know that much about her, Dove. She's been staying with Polly since June. Word around the lake is her mother's in jail. Something drug related. I don't think she even knows who her father is."

"That's rough."

"All the way around. I've got a feeling Polly's going to have her work cut out for her."

"It can't be easy. Especially at her age."

"No, it can't. But Polly's a strong, stubborn old gal. She'll manage."

"I'm taking Wendy shopping on Friday for a Halloween costume. That'll get her out of Polly's hair for the day."

"That's nice of you."

"I like Wendy. She reminds me of myself at that age."

"Speaking of Halloween, if the weather's decent tomorrow I thought I'd go out and get the pumpkins for the party. Would you like to go along?"

"It's a date."

They'd reached the cottage and she unlocked the door. Inside, Dusty lit a fire while Dove prepared a pot of coffee. Handing him a steaming cup, she sat down beside him on the couch. Her nearness was intoxicating. He took a breath.

"Dove, about last night. I don't know if I said how much I appreciate that you tried." Her eyes met his, held them. "I think it was probably my fault that we couldn't connect with her. I was afraid. Hell, I was a bundle of negative energy. I probably scared her off."

Her hand crept across the space between them, covering his. "I think we can reach her. Whenever you're ready to try again."

Maybe it was the kindness in her eyes, or the soft brush of her hand against his. All at once he was overcome with the desire to touch her. His inner voice shrieked that it was a mistake. Ignoring it, he brushed her cheek with his fingertips. "Thank you."

"For what?"

"For being you."

Her eyes held his. He was powerless to break the spell, to stop his lips from seeking hers. He kissed her gently, tasting the sweetness of her lips, savoring the moment. The kiss deepened, his hands in her hair, her hands on his shoulders, and he allowed himself to get swept away, lost in the wonder and the beauty and the magic that was Dove.

Dove. Not resisting. Not resisting at all, but quietly welcoming him in. It scared the hell out of him. "I'm sorry," he said, pulling away from her.

"Why?"

"Because I'm not—" *good enough.* The words lay between them, unstated, but no less understood.

"Shh."

She kissed him again, and he sensed an invitation lying in front of him like an unopened gift. But a gift that would lead to more pain in the end, and so he steeled himself against his desire.

"Good night Dove."

"Good night, Dusty." Disappointment clouded her eyes. The invitation was still on the table. He could feel it, see it in her beautiful eyes. He couldn't handle it, couldn't handle the desire that raged in his veins, or the fear of losing yet again. He could not handle it, and so he stood and made himself walk away.

Chapter Nine

A cold rain fell on Thursday morning, effectively dampening Dove's plans to go in search of pumpkins with Dusty. She sat at the window, watching the downpour and thinking of the kiss they'd shared. And of the ones they hadn't. She couldn't fathom the reason for his anxiety, and she hoped a night's distance had eased it.

When he stopped by the cottage at mid-morning to light a fire for her, she saw with disappointment that it hadn't. He seemed ill at ease, stilted in his speech, not quite able to meet her eyes. With a fire roaring in the grate, he made excuses for a quick getaway, and she felt as if they were back at square one, strangers again. Except that strangers didn't kiss each other the way they'd kissed. Offered like an unexpected gift, the kiss was spontaneous, but somehow, right. Cautious at first, it built like an exquisite slow-burning flame, setting her on fire.

And now he regretted it.

They owed each other nothing, still, she couldn't help feeling let down. By Dusty, and by herself. In four decades of living and loving she'd never been so disquieted by a man. Why he affected her this way, making her feel like a love-struck teenager, she couldn't say. Except that in his arms she felt at peace. In his presence she felt completely understood, completely accepted. Until last night. But dwelling on such thoughts was getting her nowhere, and so she shook the memory of his kiss from her thoughts, reminding herself she'd come to Shadow Lake to pull herself together. Passionate kisses weren't going to accomplish that, as nice as they might be.

Outside her window the wind kicked up, driving furious waves across the lake and stripping the trees of their foliage. Pouring a second cup of coffee, she turned on her laptop and began writing her final draft of the opera house story. Flipping through her photos, she selected one of Main Street after dark, hazy circles of light encircling the street lamps. Lonely and barren, the photo had an eerie, menacing feel about it and she shivered.

A month after she left Mississippi things fell apart for Wesley Wallace. With the promise of ridding the village of its evil spirits, the holy man had attempted to perform an exorcism of sorts. An email from Sammy reported that Wallace had begun by building a ring of fire around the site of the old opera house. Half the town had assembled to watch the ritual. A still, quiet night, Sammy said, but as the flames grew hotter, an unanticipated windstorm blew in, carrying the fire to the church next door. Before firefighters could contain the blaze, the church had burned to the ground, along with half of Main Street.

The townspeople were outraged. An equally irate church board of directors demanded the pastor's resignation. The news gave Dove a small measure of satisfaction. Self righteous ass. Sammy had thanked her for the help she'd given Johnna and begged Dove to return and help the other spirits. But by then she was knee-deep in the Sarah Waterman investigation and couldn't get away. In the months that passed she often wondered how things had turned out for them all.

•

She spent the remainder of the day working on her story and listening to soothing classical music. Late in the evening the power went out, plunging the cabin into dark silence. With nothing else to do, she climbed into bed, hoping the sunrise would bring a better day.

After a restless night of listening to the rain and the wailing winds, she awoke to a bright, clear morning. She was a woman who valued solitude, but after thirty-six hours inside the cabin she found herself craving human contact. After a breakfast of fried eggs and toast, she showered, dressed in a pair of well-worn jeans and a sweater, and set off for Whispering Sands Lane, pulling up in front of the blue-shingled house at nine o'clock sharp. Strolling up the cobbled walkway, she was admiring Polly's horticultural handiwork when the old woman appeared on the porch.

"Good morning, Polly."

"Good morning," Polly greeted her. "Looks like you'll have a nice day for your shopping trip."

"Yes, the weather's really shaped up nicely."

"Sunny and cool, and it's supposed to stay this way through the weekend, if the weather man can be trusted."

Dove took another moment to survey the yard and gardens. "This is a lovely place you have here. Wendy tells me you made all of these bird houses yourself."

"That's right."

"I'd love to hear about your nest box project sometime."

"Would you now?" The old woman was obviously pleased. "Maybe one day before you leave I'll put on a kettle of tea and tell you about it."

"I'll look forward to that."

The front door banged open and Wendy appeared on the porch, dressed in black jeans and a long, black coat. "Let's roll."

Polly stood on the porch, waving as they drove away.

Away from her aunt's watchful eye, Wendy's mood visibly brightened. She chattered about the upcoming party, detailing her decorating ideas for the rec hall and her plans for entertaining the children with palm readings.

"I'm going to call myself Madame Theodocia. Won't that be the bomb?"

Dove smiled. "It'll be nuclear."

An hour later they entered the West Union city limits and Wendy directed her down a seedy side street called Commerce Alley. "This is probably as close as you're going to get to Market Square," she said. "There's some big festival going on this weekend. The city's going to be mad crowded."

Pulling into the nearest lot, Dove took a ticket from the attendant and parked the car beneath a shade tree near the back.

"This costume place is way fresh," Wendy said, as they strolled through the alleyway. "I can't wait for you to see it."

Dove considered the row of derelict buildings. Commerce Alley was definitely not a place she'd want to walk alone at night. Clutching her purse a little tighter, she followed as Wendy led the way.

They cut across the alleyway and entered Market Square's west end. Once they got past the blocks of bars and pawn shops, the atmosphere turned pleasantly trendy. Coffee shops and specialty boutiques lined the sidewalks, their windows decorated with pumpkins and twinkling orange lights. The streets buzzed with activity as merchants wheeled racks of merchandise onto the sidewalks and food vendors set up shop for the day. Dove's mouth began to water as the tantalizing scents of fried dough and cold apple cider perfumed the air.

After walking several blocks they came upon a flamboyant pink building with wide purple stripes. A mint green awning sprawled across the storefront, while a sign above the door shouted: Incognito! Your One-Stop Costume shop.

Deceptively small on the outside, the store seemed to stretch for miles inside, the aisles crammed with costumes, wigs, and masquerade paraphernalia of every kind.

"Ooh, look at this," Wendy said, pulling a fawn-colored dress with dangling fringe from a rack of costumes.

"I thought you wanted to be a fortune teller."

"Not for me. For you."

Dove considered the dress. "It's not exactly what I had in mind."

"Oh, but it would be perfect."

"Do you really think so?"

"You should seriously try this on." She plowed through the rack. "What are you, like a size three?"

"I'm the same size as you." Dove thought of the cream colored dress she'd worn to Emma's wedding and hoped that she'd been mistaken in thinking it was Wendy who'd stolen it.

"Trust me, Ms. Denning," Wendy said, thrusting the dress into Dove's arms. "This costume works for you."

In the changing room, Dove slid the dress over her head. Studying her reflection in the mirror, she saw that Wendy was right. The soft fawn color complimented her olive complexion, and the suede skirt hugged her hips as if it had been custom made for her. Checking the tag, she saw that the costume was surprisingly reasonably priced. She hadn't given a thought to what she'd wear to the party. Going as a Native American princess seemed as good a plan as any.

Wendy appeared beside her in the mirror. "My God, you look gorgeous. You look just like Pocahontas."

Dove smiled. "Then I guess that settles it. Now let's see what we can find for Madame Theodocia."

After a morning-long search, during which Dove was certain Wendy would try on every costume in the entire store, she finally decided on a multi-colored, ankle-length skirt and matching scarf. On her way to the changing room she grabbed up a slinky black blouse.

"What do you think of this?" She asked, holding it up for Dove's inspection.

The blouse was low-cut and filmy to the point of being see-through. Dove winced inwardly, imagining Polly's reaction. "I love the skirt," she said. "I'm not sure the blouse is quite right, though."

Wendy's face fell. "Why not?"

"It just doesn't strike me as being authentic. Here, try this one." She grabbed up a gold peasant blouse with silver beads sprinkling the neckline and handed it to the girl.

Wendy's breath caught. "Ooh, I didn't even see that." She trotted off to the dressing room and Dove breathed a sigh of relief.

Fifteen minutes later Dove pulled out her credit card and handed it to the salesgirl. When it was her turn to pay, Wendy did the same. Seeing Dove's surprised expression, she explained, "Aunt Polly gave me her Visa card. She says I can only put fifty bucks on it, though."

After leaving the costume shop, they ducked into a shoe store, where Dove selected a pair of beaded moccasins, and Wendy, a pair of bronze, lace-up sandals.

"I don't know about you," Dove said, glancing at her watch, "but all this shopping is making me hungry."

"I know of a sweet café, but it's a little bit of a walk."

"Lead the way."

They strolled six blocks until they came to a place called The Brick House Café. Seated at a booth in an oversized window that opened onto the street, they feasted on chili dogs and potato wedges amid angst-filled music and teenagers dressed entirely in black.

"This is an interesting place," Dove commented.

"I used to come here all the time," Wendy said wistfully. "I miss this town. I hate living with Aunt Polly."

Dove bit into a potato wedge, carefully considering her words. "She doesn't seem so bad, Wendy."

"She won't let me do anything. She thinks I'm going to end up like my mom."

Before Dove could formulate a response, Wendy asked, "What's Philadelphia like?"

She swallowed a sip of water, thankful to be back on safer ground. "It's a good town. Lots of museums and history." She grinned. "Great shopping."

Wendy sighed. "Some day I'm going to live in a big city like that. I'm going to make tons of money as a tattoo artist and I'm going to have everything I want."

"A tattoo artist?"

"I like to draw and design art." She shrugged. "People say I'm pretty good at it. I figure I might as well make a living doing something I love, right?"

"You're already ahead of the game, Kiddo. It takes most people a lifetime to figure that out."

When they'd finished their meal, Dove paid the tab and they walked out into the cool, sun-drenched afternoon. It was a perfect autumn day, probably one of the last of the season and they decided to take advantage of it. Wandering through the booths at the art festival, Dove spotted a slim silver bracelet, the words Faith, Hope and Love engraved in its center. "This would look great with your costume," she said.

Wendy tried it on, admiring the way the silver gleamed in the sunlight. "Twenty bucks," she said, her expression wistful. "I'm already way over my limit."

"I'm not over mine," Dove said. "How about if I buy it for you?" The offer surprised her as much as it seemed to surprise Wendy. It wasn't like her to be impulsive, but she was enjoying Wendy's company immensely. The girl was going through a tough time, and Dove wanted to bring her a bit of happiness, if only in this small way.

Wendy removed the bracelet and set it back on the table. "I can't let you do that, Ms. Denning."

"Why not?" Digging a twenty out of her purse, Dove paid for the bracelet and steered Wendy from the booth.

"You shouldn't have done that," she protested. "Now I owe you."

"You don't owe me a thing. Thanks to you I got out of the

cabin and had a lovely day. That's well worth twenty dollars to me. Besides, we're friends, aren't we?"

Wendy gave her a hug that warmed her through and she couldn't help thinking if things had worked out differently in her life she could easily have a child Wendy's age. She indulged herself in a pleasant daydream in which Wendy was her daughter, but instead of Mark, her dream partner was Dusty.

They strolled through the square, looking at paintings and art exhibits, stopping to watch pantomime artists, magicians, and a lamp worker who fashioned a crystal rose from a piece of glass. In the center of the square a band had begun to play. A quintet of Jamaican men sang a quirky blend of reggae and hip hop while women danced in dresses of blue, purple and gold. Wendy seemed mesmerized by the sheer beauty of the dancers and the hypnotic rhythms of the music.

It was nearly five o'clock when they left the square. The air had become chilly and Dove's feet ached from a day of walking. When they finally reached the Impala, she cranked up the heater and searched in her wallet for a five-dollar bill to pay the parking fee.

"Someone left us a flyer," Wendy said, grabbing a folded sheet of paper from beneath her windshield wiper. Opening it, she frowned. "What's this supposed to mean?"

"I don't know, let me see it." Retrieving the money from her wallet, Dove shot a distracted glance at the flyer: bright red flames dancing beside a pure white cross. It was a moment before the image registered. Flames and a cross. The accursed shall be purified by fire. Oh, God. She sat for a moment, stunned.

"What's wrong?" Wendy asked.

"Shut your door."

"Why?"

"Just do it!" She spoke sharply and Wendy quickly complied. Hands trembling, she thrust the five-dollar bill through the window in the parking attendant's booth and sped out of the lot. Driving out of town, she shot frantic glances in the rearview mirror. No one followed.

"What's wrong, Ms. Denning?" Wendy asked, her earlier cheerfulness gone. Realizing she was scaring the girl, Dove pulled in a breath and tried to smile. "Nothing's wrong."

"Then why did you freak out like that?"

"I don't know. PMS, maybe."

Driving back to Shadow Lake, Dove tried to work it out in her mind. She was familiar with the symbol, the icon of the Pentecost. She'd seen it many times, and was pretty sure it commemorated the birth of the early Christian church. She tried to convince herself the flyer had been an advertisement for some sort of local church event, a tent revival, perhaps, or a concert. They'd probably printed dozens of them, left them on cars all over town. She'd gotten a defective copy, that was all. It had nothing to do with the Sam Sewall letters.

It was after six o'clock when they reached Polly's house. Darkness had long since fallen and spooky shadows seemed to hide among the trees. She glanced again in her rearview mirror. The accursed shall be purified by fire.

"Thanks for taking me today," Wendy said.

"Thanks for suggesting it," she said, forcing cheerfulness. "I had fun."

"I'll probably see you over the weekend. Me and Mick are going to get together and plan the decorations for the party."

"All right, good."

"Peace out."

She watched until Wendy was safely inside, and then drove away, her eyes sliding again to the rearview mirror. No one followed.

In the campground parking lot, she grabbed her flashlight from beneath the seat. Taking comfort in its cool, solid weight, she flipped the switch to on and hurried down the path.

Inside, her cottage was dark and quiet. She checked each room, turning on lights as she went. Satisfied that all was in order, she returned to the living room, still holding the flashlight, not letting out her breath until each door and window was securely bolted behind her.

Chapter Ten

Dusty rarely visited Chelsea's grave in the little country cemetery outside of town. As far as he was concerned, the lake was her tomb. Early mornings on the water, he felt close to her. So close that sometimes he could swear he felt the whisper of her breath against his cheek. Each sunrise was his own private memorial service, and on those mornings when the weather prevented him from going, he felt that a vital part of his day was missing.

On Friday morning, awakening to a clear, dark sky and calm winds, he set out, determined that this would be the day he would at last connect with her. Dipping his oars into the water, he paddled to his favorite spot. He spent some time listening to the quiet, readying his mind, trying to fill it with positive thoughts. As the first hints of morning colored the sky he reflected, not on his loss, but on the joy and the dynamism -- the sheer loveliness his daughter had brought to his life. He thought about Chelsea long and hard, until deep in the heart of the quiet he felt something stir.

He closed his eyes, whispered, "Honey, are you there?"

A hush fell over the lake. He concentrated on the stillness, breathing deeply, waiting for some kind of sign but none came. Tears filled his eyes and brimmed over, splashing onto his hands. He cried for the emptiness of the years they hadn't shared. Eight years stolen away in a moment of anger and hopelessness. He cried until he was empty of tears, until he felt cleansed.

He sat there long after the sun burned off the morning fog. Not ready to return home, he paddled in the opposite direction, lifting his collar against the cold, his breath leaving wisps of vapor in the air. November was coming. Soon the lake would ice over, ending his morning ritual until spring came again.

Paddling aimlessly, he came upon the abandoned bait and tackle shop. It looked desolate against the empty beach front and all at once he knew what had bothered him. He recalled Dove asking whether there'd ever been a murder there. His book said that psychics sometimes had visions of both the past and of the future. Peering at the empty windows, he tried to see if he could perceive anything sinister, but was aware only of the sun and the brisk morning air. He knew that female intuition was fallible, and he supposed the same held true of extra-sensory perception. In any case, he hoped this time Dove was wrong and nothing sinister waited on the horizon. The lake community didn't need any more trouble.

Having spiraled back to Dove, his thoughts refused to leave her. He hadn't gone back to her cottage last night to check on her when the power went out. He told himself it was because of the drenching rain, but in his heart he knew the real reason. The kiss. Like Dove, it was sensuous and lovely and full of passion. A passion he had only to ask for in order to experience, but for how long? Sooner or later she'd leave Shadow Lake. It was only a matter of time until she returned to her real life, leaving him emptier for having loved her. He couldn't, wouldn't set himself up for that kind of pain.

Throughout the day his thoughts returned to her again and again, torturing him. He daydreamed about her as he split wood, as he made his rounds through the campground, checking to see that all was in order. Trudging past her empty cabin, he felt a sharp twinge of longing. It was maddening, this tug-of-war that raged inside him. He was terrified by her and he was utterly magnetized by her. He wanted nothing to do with her, and at the same time, he wanted her to be the center of his Universe. He told himself he was glad she was away for the day, and yet, some obstinate inner demon looked forward to her return.

Thinking she might stop in after her shopping trip with Wendy, he put off dinner for as long as he could, until Mick made his way to the kitchen for the third time. He lifted the lid on the crock pot, where Dusty had started a beef stew simmering that morning.

"Dude, are we gonna eat this some time tonight?"

"Just as soon as I start the dinner rolls," he said, buying himself a few moments more.

While Mick wolfed down his dinner, Dusty pushed his food around on his plate, only half listening to the boy's nattering about some sports car or other, his ears trained for the sound of Dove's car in the driveway. When at last he heard the unmistakable crunch of tires on gravel, his gaze moved to the window. He watched her get out of the car, watched in anticipation as she glanced toward the house. But instead of moving toward it, she grabbed up a flashlight and headed down the path.

She was angry with him, then. Disappointment hit him like a sledgehammer, and he tried to tell himself it was just as well. Soon she would be gone, like his sunrise mornings on the lake. But instead of steeling his resolve, the thought made him more desperate to see her. Should he go to her, or should he push her away? The tug-of-war raged inside him. He would not give in. Drawing on every ounce of self control he possessed, he cleared away the supper dishes and stacked them in the dishwasher. He fought against the demon of desire as he swept the floor and wiped down the counter tops. He fought it until he could not fight another moment, and then he pulled on his jacket and went to her.

•

Hearing a noise, Dove moved cautiously to the window. Prying open the slats of the blinds with her fingers, she peered out, seeing only darkness. She told herself she was being overly paranoid. The flyer had been an advertisement, nothing more. But a troubling inner voice whispered that she was in danger. She'd learned long ago to trust her intuition.

A thudding sound outside sent her racing back to the window. It had started to rain again and the wind had picked up, setting the rocking chairs on the deck to bumping against the railing. She pulled in a shuddering breath, released it. It would be a long, sleepless night, each creaking floor board and every branch scraping the rooftop making her jump out of her skin. Her fear was carrying her away. What she needed was another perspective, a voice of reason. With this settled she dug her cell phone out of her purse and punched in Mark's number.

The call went to voice mail. Agitated, she paced the room. She pulled the phone out of her pocket, punched in Mark's number again. Again, the call went to voice mail. In a snap decision, she pulled her suitcases from the closet and began to throw her clothes into them. She couldn't stay here another night knowing there might be a madman out there, waiting …

Her phone rang and she grabbed it up. "Mark?"

"It's me. What's up?"

"I'm not sure. Maybe nothing." She gave him an abbreviated account of her day in the city with Wendy, and then told him about the flyer.

"Christ," he said softly. "Did anyone follow you back there?"

"No, I'm sure I wasn't followed."

"You've been there almost a week. It's unusual that he'd wait that long to make his move."

"Am I overreacting, or do you think this is related to the letters?"

"It doesn't seem likely, but let's err on the side of caution."

"If it is related to the letters, then the writer must have followed me here. Which means he's been watching me all this time, waiting for a chance to—" She began to shiver uncontrollably.

"We don't know that, Dove." He paused. "Did you happen to notice any flyers on the other cars in the lot?"

"I didn't think to look. I was so upset; all I could think about was getting the hell out of there."

"Ok, let me think."

"I'm leaving here, Mark. Tonight."

"Let me think, Dove." After a moment's silence he said, "Look, it's already after seven, that's going to make it awfully late for you to be on the road and I don't like the idea of you driving alone. Is there anyone there that could stay with you tonight?"

She thought fleetingly of Dusty. She wouldn't even dare to suggest such a thing after last night. "No."

"All right. I'll head up there then. We'll ride back together in the morning."

"I don't want you to do that, Mark."

"I'd feel better if there was someone there with you."

"It's a long drive and it's late. I guess I could ask Dusty if I can stay in the cabin tonight. I'm sure he wouldn't mind if I used the couch for one night."

"I think we'd both sleep a lot better if you did. When you get back home I'll have someone shadow you. Let me make a few calls and see who's available for surveillance for the next few days."

"It seems a lot of trouble if it was just a coincidence."

"Better safe than sorry, babe. Call me if you need me. Otherwise I'll talk to you first thing in the morning."

She disconnected the call, her fears slightly eased. Even so, she couldn't keep herself from checking the windows again. Rechecking the dead bolt on the door, she heard a determined knock. She froze in indecision, her heart hammering. The knock came again, more forcefully. Creeping to the window, she peeled back the blinds and peeked out. Dusty stood on the front porch. With a shudder of relief, she opened the door.

"You didn't stop in tonight," he said. "I thought I'd come by and see if..." his voice trailed away as his gaze rested on her open suitcases. "You're leaving?"

"I'm sorry, Dusty. It looks like I might have to."

"Dove, if it's about last night, I ..."

"It's not about last night."

"Then what is it about?"

"Come inside."

Retrieving her purse from the counter, she pulled out the flyer and handed it to him. "It's about this."

He studied it before lifting his eyes to hers. "I don't understand."

"I need a drink." In the kitchen, she opened the bottle of Chablis she'd picked up in town and poured herself a glass. Carrying it back to the living room, she settled beside him on the sofa. He watched her intently, waiting for an explanation.

She took a long swallow from her glass. "Earlier this summer I was involved in a murder investigation. A young girl. Her name was Sarah ..." The words were painful and she choked on them. His hand moved to her back, making slow, soothing circles and she forced the words out. "Sarah was everything a young girl should be. Smart, pretty, talented. Truly gifted."

"In what way?"

"She could prophesy. She foretold certain current events, mostly having to do with the conflict in the Middle East." She reached for her wine, took another swallow. "In early June Sarah was brutally murdered. The chief investigator was my ex-husband, Mark Denning. Since Sarah had extrasensory gifts, he thought I might be able to help, so I went out to the murder scene. Day after day,

I went out there." Tears trickled down her face as she stopped to compose herself. "The moment I arrived I could feel residual traces of her terror. The air was positively black with malevolence. I knew that whatever happened there, it had been horrible. I'd never felt anything that strongly. The evil that lingered in that crime scene ... it made me physically ill."

She sat, quietly reliving the memory. "Even so, I went back. Again and again, I went back. I wanted justice for that girl, for Sarah, and little by little, the occurrence began to show itself to me."

"You saw the murderer?" he asked.

"Not his face. I saw images. A dark sedan, a blue and yellow necktie. From the first I sensed very strongly that it was someone Sarah knew, someone she trusted. At that point the murder scene was pretty much a pile of smoldering ruins, but they found trace evidence. Eight weeks later they arrested one of the church deacons."

"Good God."

"It came out at the trial that he was infatuated with Sarah. They found pictures of her in his house. He obsessed over her day and night, and finally in his madness, he convinced himself that she was a witch."

Dusty's breath whistled through his teeth. "Christ."

"Shortly after the trial ended I got a letter. The words had been cut out of a magazine and pasted together, like those threatening letters you used to see in old mystery movies.

"What did it say?"

"It said, 'Be not deceived! Evil will be hunted down and destroyed wherever it is found. There shall not be among you any that use divination, nor any enchanters, nor those who consult with spirits, nor any witches. For those who do these things are an abomination unto the Lord: and He shall drive them out from before you. The land shall be purged of wickedness. The accursed shall be purified by fire.' I'd gotten some strange correspondence after the trial. I thought it was just another weirdo. But then a few days later I got another letter."

He faced her, his expression grim. "What did that one say?"

"It said, 'The hunt is on.' Both letters were signed Samuel Sewall."

"I don't understand. He signed his name?"

"Samuel Sewall was a judge in the Salem Witch trials back in the sixteen hundreds. The Deacon was safely behind bars, so I assumed the letter was written by someone who'd followed the story closely. Maybe even someone from the same church." She drained her glass. "It's strange, though. None of the women in Salem were burned. They were hanged. Oh, God." She began to tremble and tears streamed from her eyes. "Sarah Waterman was burned alive."

He pulled her to him, his expression fierce. "I'm not going to let anything happen to you, Dove. You can stay at the house with Mick and I until Shane and Emma get back. Then we'll figure something else out."

"I can't ask you to baby-sit me twenty-four/seven. I think I should head back to Philly."

Pure longing flickered in his eyes. "I wish you'd stay," he said softly.

She barely dared breathe. "Why?"

"Because I want to know you're safe." His hands traced a slow path down her spine, a simple gesture of comfort that started a slow fire burning inside her. She turned her face to his kiss and the flame ignited. She clung to the safety and the strength and the goodness of him, as if his very presence could keep the evil at bay. His touch had set her on fire, and yet she shivered in anticipation as his lips moved to her neck, as his hands slid beneath the softness of her sweater, giving pleasure and heat. Exquisite, all-consuming heat. It consumed her as her hands found his zipper. Torturous, breathless heat as their garments fell, unneeded to the floor. He whispered her name, clearly a question. And in answer, she took his hand and led him to the bedroom.

Unquenchable fire burned within her, and yet she was at sea, adrift on wave after wave of desire as he explored her body. As she explored his. Each in desperate need, their bodies melded together until every trace of ugliness and doubt vanished and only the beauty of their union remained.

Afterward, she fell asleep and dreamed of Sarah Waterman. She woke up sobbing and Dusty held her close to his heart. Feeling his eyes on her in the dark, she burrowed against him, seeking comfort in the warmth and the steadiness of him. She'd always thought of herself as strong, had always prided herself on her resourcefulness. But just as her father had kept watch over her mother, she felt reassured in knowing this man watched over her. This was her last conscious thought, as nestling deeper into the safe circle of his arms, she drifted back to sleep.

Chapter Eleven

On Saturday morning Dusty awoke from a beautiful dream feeling as though he was living one. He considered the woman who lay beside him, her face hidden in the shadows, and felt a sublime sense of joy, an aliveness he hadn't felt in years, if ever. The moment would have been perfect if not for the underlying sense of impending danger.

The hunt is on …

Thoughts of Dove's stalker started a ferocious anger burning inside him. He'd made a promise to keep her safe. It was a promise he'd keep, no matter what it took.

Moving carefully so as not to disturb her, he pushed back the blankets and climbed out of bed. Shivering in the chilly morning air, he walked to the living room, where his clothes were tangled up with Dove's on the floor. He pulled them on before quietly letting himself out, taking care to lock the door behind him.

His rowboat bobbed gently in the water beside the dock, waiting for him. Not wanting to stray too far from where Dove slept, he sat down on the jetty instead. The lake seemed uneasy that morning. Pockets of turbulence swirled beneath its glassy surface, as if mirroring his own conflicting emotions. Somewhere in the distance, the call of a loon disrupted the morning stillness. As the sun began its slow ascent, he watched its glorious color spread across the sky and waited for his usual sense of peace, but that morning he could not calm his racing thoughts. He ached to return to the warm bed they'd shared. To return to Dove.

He sat until his face burned with cold, then reluctantly stood and headed for home. After a shower and a change of clothes, he set about preparing breakfast. Thirty minutes later, coaxed from sleep by the scents of bacon and eggs, Mick appeared in the kitchen.

"Good morning," Dusty greeted him.

"Morning." He poured a glass of orange juice and took his place at the table. "Is everything okay with Ms. Denning?"

Dusty raised his eyes from the fry pan. "Why do you ask?"

Mick dropped his gaze to the table, and with a shrug, said, "You stayed down there kind of late last night."

Damn. He'd hoped Mick hadn't noticed. Kids grew up much more quickly now than they had when he was young, and though he sensed no hint of disapproval in the boy, an old fashioned sense of propriety made him want to protect Dove, even in this.

"Keeping tabs on me?" he said, his tone light.

"Naw, Dude, nothing like that. It's just that we usually watch the Monster Truck Tour on Friday nights. I thought you'd be back in time. It's no big deal."

Dusty considered his options. He definitely couldn't tell Mick everything. Still, he had to tell him something. Deciding quickly, he told him about the letters and about the flyer, glossing over the more disturbing details. When he'd finished, Mick stared at him, wide eyed. "Wendy said she got kind of weird yesterday. Holy crap, now I can see why."

"With all that's going on I think it would be best if she stayed up here with us until your father and Emma get back. Just to make sure nothing happens."

"Nothing will," he said, his voice oozing teenaged confidence. "Not on my watch."

"I'm glad you feel that way."

"I don't get it, Dusty. Who would want to hurt a good person like Ms. Denning?"

Dusty sighed. "I wish I knew, kid."

At nine o'clock he returned to the cottage to find Dove awake and talking on her cell phone. He poured himself a cup of coffee and carried it to the living room, doing his best not to eavesdrop on her half of the conversation. It didn't take long for him to realize she was speaking with her ex-husband, Mark Denning. Overcome with irrational jealousy, he stared out the window, fidgeting with his coffee cup, until finally she addressed him.

"Dusty, Mark would like to talk to you."

Clearing his throat, he took the phone from her hand. "Hello?"

"Good morning. Dove tells me she's going to be staying with you for awhile?"

It was an honest question, asked in a straightforward, if not friendly, manner. Still, he felt awkward as hell. "That's right."

"I think that might be the wisest course of action. We're short on manpower, and there's no one available to stay with her full time. That's what she'll need, at least for the time being."

"No one's going to get near her here. I can promise you that."

"That makes me feel a whole lot better, Dusty. Listen, I'm not sure who we're dealing with, if anyone at all. I told Dove that if she should see or hear anything strange, or even if something just doesn't feel quite right, she's to call the police. And then call me. I'd like you to do the same."

"You got it."

He disconnected the call and handed the phone back to Dove. She smiled. "I guess it's official, then. You're my new baby sitter."

"I'm not your baby sitter, Dove. I'm your friend."

"Just a friend?"

The moment was electrically charged and he felt himself start to sweat. Two short beeps sounded outside, precluding an answer.

"That's Mick with the golf cart. He's going to help us move your things up to the house."

Walking behind the golf cart as it moved ahead of him up the path, he would have given anything to have that moment back. To tell her how he really felt.

•

When she'd stowed her food items in the fridge, Dove followed Dusty down the hallway to Shane and Emma's bedroom, where Mick had already deposited the rest of her belongings. Her glance swept over the cherry wood bed with its wedding ring quilt, the silver-framed photos of Shane and Emma on the night stand and dressers. White lace curtains fell softly over a pair of wooden shutters in the window, effectively shutting out the world. The room was a tasteful and comfortable retreat, a love nest.

She turned to Dusty, who stood watching her intently. "Are you sure they won't mind?"

"They won't mind." He shifted his weight from foot to foot. "Dove, about last night."

She held up her hand. "I don't want to analyze it, Dusty. It was beautiful and incredible and I'm glad it happened."

"I'm glad it happened, too."

"Are you?"

"I'm sorry if I don't know quite how to act. It's been a long time for me."

"Me too. But I've learned not to look back." She gazed into his eyes, wondering if there was a way to go forward.

"Then I'll try to do the same." He took a step toward her. Just as she was certain the moment would end in a kiss, Mick poked his head in the door.

"Hey, guys. Am I, like, interrupting a moment?"

"Of course not," Dusty said. "What do you need?"

"I just got a text from Wendy. She wants to know if we're still going to get the pumpkins today."

A half hour later the truck bumped along the lake road, Dusty and Dove in the front, with Mick and Wendy settled into the back. Though the day was chilly, the sky was a cloudless blue and Dove's uneasiness from the previous day began to fade.

After a number of twists in the road, they pulled into a rutted lot beneath a brightly painted sign that said: *Welcome to Crabtree Farms.* A pole barn with a red tin roof sat at the edge of the lot, crates of squash and cabbage stacked up beside tables displaying breads, pies and other fresh-baked goods. Beside the store, a brown field seemed to stretch for miles, scattered with orange and yellow pumpkins of every size imaginable.

"This is the place," Dusty said, shutting off the engine.

While Mick and Wendy went to explore the pumpkin patch, she and Dusty wandered through the store, selecting gourds, Indian corn and jars of peach and blackberry preserves.

"Hello, Dusty." A stout woman of approximately Dusty's age appeared from out of nowhere. Startled, Dove nearly dropped the jar of honey she'd been holding. Dusty placed a reassuring hand on her arm.

"'Morning, Glenda. Beautiful day."

"That it is. Getting all ready for your big party next weekend?"

"We're getting there. We came to clean out your pumpkin patch."

Her curious glance swept over Dove.

"Glenda, this is my friend, Dove."

"Nice to meet ya." She turned her gaze back to Dusty. "Finding everything, then?"

"Actually, I didn't see any battery operated torches. You know, the ones we used last year to light the paths for the hayride?"

"Sold all I had to a gentleman that came in yesterday morning. Strange duck. Said he was having a private party on the lake. I can put some on order, though. Should have them by the middle of the week."

"Let me know as soon as they come in, will you?"

"Will do." Her glance crept back to Dove before resting once again on Dusty. "Let me know if you need help with the cookies this year. I have a new recipe and a couple of free afternoons this week."

"We'll need a bunch of them. Give Polly Church a call. She's organizing the baking party."

The woman's lips pursed, as if she were miffed. "I'll do that, Dusty."

Back outside, Dove smiled at him. "Is there anyone around here you don't know?"

"Not many."

"It must be nice, living in a community where everyone's so neighborly."

"Neighborly." He chuckled. "I think the word you want is nosy. Sometimes I think the anonymity of the city would be heaven."

The comment sparked an idea and Dove set it aside to think about later. "The kids work fast," she said, indicating the two piles of pumpkins that sat beside the truck. Out in the field, Mick seemed intent on collecting the biggest pumpkins he could find, while Wendy carefully considered the size and shape of each one before making a commitment.

"I know nothing about picking out pumpkins," Dove confessed.

"Nothing much to it," Dusty said, folding her hand in his. "Just grab whichever ones strike your fancy."

An hour later, with the bed of the truck nearly filled, they went back inside for complimentary cider and donuts while Glenda tallied their purchases. "We'll make it an even seventy-five, same discount as always," she told Dusty. "Want me to just send the bill to the campground?"

"Please."

"All-righty then, you're all set."

"Thanks, Glenda."

"I'll give Polly a call about the cookies."

"You do that."

Back at the campground, they lugged the pumpkins inside the rec hall. "What a lot of work," Dove said, surveying the mountains of orange.

"You ain't seen nothing yet," Mick said with a grin. "Wait 'till it's time to carve them."

"Which would be now." Dusty went to the house, returning with a stack of old newspapers and a set of kitchen knives. "All right Mick. Let's show the lady how this is done."

He demonstrated how to cut off the top and scoop out the pulpy insides.

"This is so gross." Wendy made a face as she scooped the insides from her pumpkin. "I think the girls should cut off the tops and let the guys do the scooping. What do you think, Ms. Denning?"

"I think you're being a wuss," Mick said.

"I am not!"

Scooping a handful of pulp from his pumpkin, he flung it at her and she squealed.

Dusty put a CD of Halloween music on the boom box and they all got down to business, Wendy carving intricate designs in her pumpkins, while Dove hacked out basic triangles. She loved every minute of it, loved Mick's good-natured jokes at her expense and the way Dusty's eyes slid to hers, conveying warmth and shared secrets. As the afternoon slipped away, so did the last traces of her fear and she was glad she'd decided to stay. Surrounded by the carefree laughter of youth and with romance blossoming in the air, anything at all seemed possible and trouble seemed a million miles away.

Chapter Twelve

Monday morning the slamming of the front door pulled Dove from a deep, delicious sleep. Disoriented by the darkness and the unfamiliar room, she groped beside her for the bedside clock. Clearing the cobwebs from her brain, she peered at the glowing dial. *Six forty-five. Dear God.*

Groaning, she pulled the sheets around her in a warm cocoon and tried to slide back into oblivion, but the scent of strong, rich coffee invaded her senses and pulled her from the bed. The chill morning air embraced her like an unwanted lover and she dressed quickly in jeans and a heavy sweater before heading out to start her day.

Finding the kitchen empty, she helped herself to a cup of coffee, sat down at the table, and leafed through the Penny Saver that had arrived the day before. On the second page, a bold, black and orange advertisement for the campground's Halloween party caught her eye.

Join Us for the Fifth Annual
Halloween Spooktacular at Shadow Lake Campground!
Bring your little ghosts and gremlins for an evening of fun!
Apple bobbing • Haunted Hayride • Games •
Refreshments • Prizes
Party Starts at 6:00 p.m.
Adult Party to Follow at 9:00 p.m.
Music • Costumes • Prizes
All are Welcome • Admission is Free!

Beautifully done, the ad was embellished with grinning ghouls and comical black cats in pointed hats. Flipping through the pages, she read ads for upcoming festivals, pancake breakfasts, and a Harvest Dance sponsored by the United Methodist Church. It all seemed so cozy and down-home and she couldn't help smiling, feeling as far removed from her real life as if she'd landed on another planet.

She was finishing her second cup of coffee when Dusty walked through the back door, glowing with fresh air and masculinity. With a glance at him her stomach fluttered like a moth in the lamp light.

"Did Mick wake you when he left?" he asked. "I swear that kid doesn't know how to close a door quietly."

"Your coffee woke me. But it's all right. I had to get up anyway."

He poured a cup and joined her at the table. "Got plans for the day?"

"There are still an awful lot of pumpkins left to be carved."

"Mick's having some friends over after school to finish them up. Actually, I was hoping you'd help me get the trails ready for the hayride."

They lingered at the table, engaging in comfortable conversation. With their coffee finished, she followed him outside to the storage barn, where he studied the array of tools that hung from a peg board above the work bench. "You any good with a chain saw?" he asked.

"Not hardly."

"I thought not." He grinned and handed her a set of loppers and a pair of sturdy brown work gloves. Outside, a John Deere tractor gleamed in the morning sun, a home made trailer hitched behind it. Dusty laid the tools in the trailer beside a large cardboard box. "Your chariot," he said, indicating the trailer.

"I'm riding in that?"

"Another first?"

"Definitely."

He winked. "Stick with me, Babe."

I intend to. The thought came to her unawares, startling her with its intensity. She climbed into the trailer, gripping its sides as the tractor rumbled down the path. Within moments they detoured and headed down a wide trail that Dove hadn't known existed. They followed its zigzag pattern through the woods, stopping to cut back overhanging branches and throw them into the trailer. They'd take them back to the campground and chip them up, Dusty explained, to use for mulch in the spring.

The loppers felt heavy and awkward in her hands. After a half hour, her shoulders ached and angry blisters rose on her hands despite the heavy work gloves. She stopped to massage an aching knot between her shoulder blades.

"Ready for a break?" Dusty asked.

"Whenever you are."

They seated themselves on the back of the trailer and Dusty handed her a bottle of flavored water. She uncapped it and took a generous swallow. "So, tell me about this hayride of yours."

He shrugged. "It started one year as an afterthought and now it's the highlight of the party. The first year it was just some spider webs and skeletons hanging in the trees. The next year Shane decided to have a couple of older kids dress up as ghosts and jump out at the kids. Last year he added a fake graveyard. The spooks are of the cartoon variety, though. Just fun stuff. We don't want to scare the little ones too badly."

"How far do you go?"

"A couple of miles. There's a big open field up ahead. I usually turn around there and head back. All in all it takes about forty minutes."

"Sounds like fun."

He regarded her thoughtfully. "Never been on a hayride, either?"

"Nope."

"I'll have you come with me, then. You can sit in the wagon and keep an eye on the little ones."

"I'd love that."

"Then it's a date." He squeezed her hand, and she felt the unmistakable rhythm of sexual energy pulsing between them.

An hour later, with the path cleared of limbs, Dusty drove into a large open field and turned off the tractor. "This is as far as we go," he told her. "I thought I'd set up the graveyard today, as long as we're here."

Removing half a dozen crosses from the back of the trailer, he carried them to the shade of a large maple tree and set about pounding them into the ground.

"What can I do to help?" she asked.

"There are more decorations in that box in the trailer. You can set them around, if you want."

Opening the flaps, she saw the box was filled with life-sized wooden cutouts of headstones, Jack O' Lanterns, and spooky black cats.

"These are adorable."

"Wendy painted those up for us last week."

She carried the cut outs to the makeshift graveyard and arranged them beside the crosses, admiring her young friend's considerable talent.

As she worked, a shadow seemed to cross the sun and she shivered. Standing back, she shaded her eyes with her hand and peered across the field into the ring of trees that encircled the meadow. They swayed in the gentle breeze, their naked branches echoing with bird song. Her hair prickled at the nape of her neck despite her tranquil surroundings. There was something out there, watching them. She could feel its energy flowing in their direction. Whether animal or spiritual, she couldn't say, but she definitely detected ill will. She turned to Dusty, wondering whether he sensed it as well. He didn't seem to.

"All set?" he asked, pounding the last stake into the ground.

"Uh-huh," she said, clutching her sweater close around her.

"Are you cold?"

She shot another glance into the trees, shivered again. "Maybe just a little."

"Here." He removed his jacket and draped it across her shoulders. "Let's head back. It's got to be getting close to lunch time."

She climbed into the trailer, not looking back as the tractor rumbled toward home.

Back at the cabin she prepared tomato soup and a plate of grilled cheese sandwiches. The sun streamed through the windows, lending a feeling of warmth and safety and she found herself humming as she worked.

"That's a good job done," Dusty said, taking his place at the table. "Tomorrow morning I'll go up and bush hog the field and set the torches along the paths. If Glenda gets them in time, that is."

"Wake me up early. I'll go and help you."

"Actually, Dove, I got a call from Polly this morning. Some of the women from the community are coming up to bake cookies tomorrow for the party. It might be more fun for you to stay here and help them."

She grinned. "A country bake-off. That'll be another first for me."

"I think you'll enjoy it. They're a good group of girls." He chuckled. "Just don't tell them anything you don't want the whole town to know."

With the meal finished, they stacked the dirty dishes in the dishwasher.

"What's this?" Noticing her blisters, he gently took her hand in his.

"Just a couple of blisters. No big deal."

Retrieving a jar of salve from the cupboard, he led her back to the table and worked a dab into her palm. His touch was electric, erotic in its gentleness.

"So," she asked, "What's next on the agenda, Boss?"

He replaced the lid on the jar. "I think we've done all we need to for today."

"I can think of one other thing."

He lifted his eyes to hers. "And what would that be?"

"What time does Mick get home?"

"Three-thirty or so." A smiled tugged at the corners of his mouth. "Why do you ask?"

She smiled.

"Ms. Denning, are you trying to proposition me?"

Sliding from her chair, she climbed onto his lap, her legs straddling his hips. "I wouldn't dream of it," she said, playfully nipping his ear.

Pulling her closer, he kissed her, a deep and hungry kiss, all traces of his earlier self consciousness gone. Lifting her effortlessly, he carried her to the bedroom and eased her down onto the bed. They took their time undressing each other, tasting, exploring each other's bodies until she was trembling with desire.

"You're a beautiful woman, Dove Denning," he whispered.

"And you are a beautiful man, Dusty Martin."

Kissing, touching, each moment sweet torture until at last he entered her. Their bodies merged in a singular blend of pleasure, need and greed. Welcoming it all, it occurred to her that he wasn't just making love to her, he was completing her.

Afterward, they lay, spent, in each other's arms.

"Love in the afternoon," she murmured, snuggled against him. "I can't remember the last time I had that kind of time."

"I never had that kind of opportunity."

She looked at him in surprise. "But you were married."

"My wife wasn't big on afternoon sex. Or any kind of sex at all, as far as that goes."

She smiled. "She didn't know what she was missing."

He stroked her hair.

They lay quietly, the afternoon sunlight streaming in the window. "It's like a different world here, a different life. In my real life on a Monday afternoon I'd be racing in five different directions all at once. This is a nice change of pace."

"I'm going to be awfully sorry to see you go back to Philadelphia."

"You could come with me," she said, surprising herself as much as him.

He gazed at her intently. "And do what once I got there?"

"It's a big town. And you're very capable. I'm sure we could find you something."

"Dove," he said, softly stroking her cheek. "I'm too old pick up and start again." He kissed her. "But I love that you asked me to."

•

Lying alone in the big bed that night, Dove played the conversation back in her mind. She shouldn't have suggested such a thing to him and couldn't imagine now why she had. *Because you love him*, an inner voice whispered.

She spent a long moment in analyzing the thought. Dusty Martin had all of the qualities she admired in a man. He was kind and hard working and honest. Reliable to a fault. Simply put, she felt safe with him.

She'd never needed a man before. Not even Mark. Not really. But she sensed that Dusty was the kind of man a woman could get lost in without losing her own identity. When she was with Dusty she felt whole, as if, in finding him, she'd also found a vital part of herself she hadn't even known was missing. If that wasn't the definition of love, she didn't know what was. Still, she couldn't ask him to rearrange his whole life, any more than she could rearrange hers. So what could they do?

She considered a dozen scenarios with a dozen possible outcomes, until such thoughts exhausted her. Sometime in the dark of night she felt a subtle shift taking place inside her, altering her, until as tangibly as the autumn winds that howled outside her window, she could hear the faint whispers of change beginning to blow through her life.

Chapter Thirteen

The week before the party passed in a bittersweet blend of frantic morning activity and long, lazy afternoons of lovemaking. Dove savored every moment she spent with Dusty, knowing that soon she would have to leave this magical world behind and return to reality. And she would have to return alone.

On Saturday morning a veil of thick, gray clouds blanketed the sky and the first, wispy snowflakes of the season swirled softly above the lake. As if the darkness had found its way inside her soul as she slept, Dove awakened with an uneasy sense of foreboding. It wasn't the usual disquiet she felt over her impending departure from Shadow Lake. It was something much more ominous. Sitting upright on the side of the bed, she pulled in deep, cleansing breaths. She searched the quiet, waiting to see what, if anything, the universe would tell her. After several moments the feeling passed. Pulling on jeans and a sweater, she walked through the empty house, silent except for the ticking of the clock on the kitchen wall. Another wave of anxiety threatened and she shook it off, attributing it to the dreary weather.

The frigid air stole her breath away as she stepped outside and hurried across the lot to the rec hall. Despite the gloom outside, the hall buzzed with happy activity as last minute preparations were being put in place for the party. Some of the permanent campers had returned for the gala event, and it looked as though Dusty had recruited them to help string the yards of black crepe paper streamers and twinkling orange lights he'd bought. She moved to the center of the room, where a dance platform had been erected. Above it, dozens of miniature spiders hung suspended from shimmering gossamer webs.

Her glance traveled to a far corner, where Wendy and Mick bickered good-naturedly as they set up Madame Theodocia's fortune telling booth. At a banquet table in the back, Polly and Glenda frosted the last of the pumpkin cut-out cookies they'd baked earlier in the week.

Not finding Dusty inside, she wandered out to the storage barn and found him busily filling the trailer with hay. The edginess she'd felt only moments before dissolved in his presence. Stealing up behind him, she wrapped her arms around his waist.

"Good morning."

"Hey." He pulled her into his arms and kissed her. "I was going to let you sleep in this morning."

"What time did you get up?"

"Sometime between three and four."

"Good Lord. Have you been out here all this time? I was going to help decorate."

"You'll need your rest for the party tonight."

"I hope the weather clears up." She gathered her jacket closer around her. "I can't believe it's actually snowing in October."

"Wouldn't be the first time it snowed on Halloween. Or even the second." He smiled. "Don't worry. It'll take more than a few snowflakes to keep the lake folks away. We might have to make it a covered wagon hayride, that's all."

"Do you think we'll still draw a big crowd?"

"Big enough. It's usually a pretty tame event, though." He tossed a new hay bale into the wagon. "I hired a couple off duty cops, just in case."

"In case of what?"

He shrugged. "Some of the locals can get a little carried away."

He wouldn't meet her eyes, and she knew that at least part of the reason was the unresolved threat that still hovered in the air around her. But she didn't want to think about that today.

"What can I do to help you?"

"You could staple some streamers to the sides of the trailer."

Retrieving two large rolls of black and orange streamers from the work bench, she set about draping the sides of the wagon while Dusty padded the bed with hay bales, and as a finishing touch, added a grinning, life-sized scarecrow.

"That ought to do it," he said, standing back to survey his

handiwork.

"It's adorable."

"You're adorable," he said, planting another kiss on her lips. "I should run into town now. I have to get some gas for the tractor, and pick up the donuts for tonight."

"Hurry back."

She watched as the truck disappeared down the road, then returned to the rec hall, where Glenda was assembling goodie bags. "Want some help?" she asked.

"I'd love it, hon." She indicated the array of spider rings, candies, and Halloween pencils that were laid out on the table. "Each of these bags gets one of each item. When you've filled them, tie them off with this orange ribbon. Got it?"

She was as serious as a brain surgeon, and Dove couldn't help chuckling. "Got it."

As Dove filled the bags, Glenda scurried away, another task to see to.

The rest of the day passed in a dizzying flurry of activity as Dove polished apples, prepared apple cider punch, and set up a game corner, complete with a pumpkin piñata and pin the tail on the black cat. By five o'clock the storm clouds had blown away and a bright orange moon lit the sky. After a supper of pepperoni pizza and Buffalo style chicken wings, Dove and Wendy retreated to the bedroom to change into their costumes. Caught up in the festive atmosphere of the day, Dove forgot her earlier trepidation. She felt a flutter of excitement as she slipped into the suede Indian princess dress. Across the room, Wendy struggled with her own costume.

"Ugh. I must have gained a bazillion pounds since we went shopping. Is this top too tight?"

Dove's glance skimmed over the girl's bulging blouse. "I think it would fit a lot better if you removed some of the padding. What have you got in there, an entire package of socks?"

"I don't have anything in there," she insisted.

"Give them up, girlfriend," Dove said, holding out her hand.

Rolling her eyes, Wendy reached inside her blouse and removed a wad of paper towels.

"Much better."

Pouting, the girl studied her reflection. "Do you think Mick will like me in this?"

"You look gorgeous, Wendy."

Tearing her gaze from the mirror, she looked at Dove for the first time. "Wowsers, so do you. Dusty will flip when he sees you in that."

"Let me give you a piece of advice, kiddo. Don't ever dress for a man. Dress for yourself."

"I know. I'm just saying ..."

Dove ran a brush through her hair, then parted it in the center and braided each side. Satisfied that her look was complete, she turned from the mirror. "We should head over. It's nearly six."

They hurried across the lot, which was already filling with cars. Small children dressed as everything from angels to action heroes scurried across the lot, their pumpkin baskets swinging as they went. Entering the rec hall, Dove was pleasantly surprised to see that many of the parents had come in costume, as well. There were Raggedy Anne's and Andy's, Scooby Do's and mermaids, even a family dressed up as a set of Crayola crayons. Within moments of Wendy's arrival, a line of little girls was queued up at the fortune telling booth. Dove smiled, watching Wendy slip into her persona.

"Velcome to Madame Theodocia's," she said, affecting a thick accent. "Come, sit. Hear your fortune."

The awed little girls hung on her every word as they followed her inside. Across the room, Mick, dressed as a Mohawk Indian complete with war paint, assembled a gathering of little boys for a game of 'ghost, ghost, goose!' Sporting a scarecrow costume, Dusty manned the refreshments table. Smiling again, she walked over to him.

"You look stunning," he said, handing her a glass of punch.

"You're not so bad, yourself." She took a swallow of the sweet liquid. "Looks like the party's off to a fabulous start."

"So far, so good." He chuckled as raucous little boy shouts came from the game corner. "At least the cops are here, in case the crowd gets out of hand."

"They're here already? I didn't think a police presence would be required just yet."

"Actually, they're in Dad mode. You see Batman over there?" He indicated a large man in a caped crusader mask leading a game of pin the tail on the black cat. "That's Officer Joe MacGowan. The miniature Hanna Montana over there is his daughter, and The

Joker is his wife, Julia. Spiderman's around here somewhere. That would be Mack Frazier. He's probably off looking for the donuts."

"Looks like you've got all your bases covered, Boss."

"I'm going to go and work the crowd. Can I get you to set up the apple bobbing tank?"

"I'd be delighted."

From there, the evening flew by on the wings of fun and laughter. Dove supervised the apple bobbing competition, and then helped Mick and Wendy judge the costume contest, awarding first prize to a little girl dressed as Dora the Explorer. At eight o'clock, Dusty assembled the eager children for the hayride. Dove settled into the wagon with them, relieved to be off her aching feet.

The air was exhilarating as the wagon moved slowly down the path, the stars twinkling like ten thousand points of light in the night sky. The electric torches had arrived that morning, and now bathed the trails in golden light, lending a magical feeling to the evening.

The children huddled together in the wagon, blissfully terrified as the trees swayed eerily around them. A little princess of four or five snuggled against Dove's side, and once again she felt a pang of sadness at her decision to abstain from motherhood.

"Tell us a ghost story, tell us a ghost story!" they chorused.

Having been forewarned that spook stories were a part of the protocol, she was prepared for the request.

"On a dark and spooky night, a little girl with long, blonde curls went out for a walk in the woods."

"Why?" a little boy asked, horrified.

"Because she was going to visit her grandmother on the other side of the forest."

"Just like Little Red Riding Hood?"

"Yes, just like that," Dove said, smiling. "As she was walking, she heard a rustling sound in the trees behind her."

"Who was it?" they asked in unison.

"It was a little black cat ..."

She meandered through the story, enjoying her audience's reaction more than she would have thought possible. As the wagon neared the entrance to the field, she delivered the ending.

"And just as she reached the edge of the forest, all of the little kittens jumped out and hollered ..."

"Boo!" Mick and his friend Boots sprung from the brush, arms flapping, causing the children to shriek with fear and delight.

They passed through a gate guarded by two glow-in-the-dark skeletons, their grinning faces mere inches from the wagon. The children squealed again and Dove laughed. As the tractor moved around a loop lit by torches, she could see the beady black eyes of the rubber bats they'd hidden in the trees. Glancing toward the graveyard, she saw the grinning cats and the gleaming headstones she and Dusty had erected and braced herself for another onslaught of children's screams. Looking closer, she saw that something else had been added to the display. She peered into the distance, trying to see what it was. A finger of fear traced down her spine and she shivered.

"Tell us another story!" the children begged.

"Once upon a time ..."

The words stuck in her throat as the graveyard came into full view and she saw clearly what had been added to their display. Suspended from the branches of the maple tree, a mannequin swayed from the end of a hangman's noose. Its long, dark hair fluttered in the breeze, a witch's hat perched crookedly on its head. She stared in horror, not able to believe what she was seeing.

At the mannequin's feet, dozens of electric torches were piled like logs on a fire, and their golden orange flames seemed to lick at the hem of the mannequin's gown—a sheer, cream colored gown with elaborate bead work and intricately embroidered edges.

The gown she had bought for Emma's wedding.

Dusty bumped the tractor up to full throttle and the children shrieked.

"Turn away from it, Dove," he shouted. But she couldn't hear him above the rumbling tractor and the sound of her blood pounding through her veins.

The mannequin's head was tilted at a grotesque angle, its hands bent and holding a sign: *The Wages of Sin.*

The children shrieked again and Dusty shouted to be heard above them. "Dove, honey, it's all right."

But it wasn't all right. She was trembling, her pulse fluttering, like the mannequin fluttering in the flickering flames. And then an owl raised its haunting cry in the moonlight, and her breath came back to her and she screamed.

Chapter Fourteen

Back at the campground, Dusty lifted the children out of the wagon and then climbed inside and scrambled to the back, where Dove sat huddled against a bale of hay. Without a word he pulled her into his arms. Trembling, she collapsed against him.

"I'm so sorry," he said softy.

"He's here."

"I'm not going to let anything happen to you, Dove. You have my word."

"I have to leave, Dusty. Right now. Tonight."

"Listen to me." He took her face in his hands. "I know you're scared, but you said yourself that Philadelphia is a big city. He'll get swallowed up in the confusion there, hide out in some dark alley, and wait for another chance to ..." His voice cracked. "This is a small community. We can find him here."

Mick bounded up to the wagon. "That was so awesome! Did you hear those kids scream when we ..." Sensing the somber tone of the moment, he broke off in mid-sentence. "What's wrong?"

"Mick, did you see anyone out there while you were hiding? Anyone at all?"

"No, why? What happened?"

Dusty sighed. "There's a mannequin hanging from a rope in the maple tree out in the field. She's wearing Dove's dress."

Dove moaned softly and Dusty gathered her closer.

"No way," Mick said.

"Go and get McGowan and Frazier. Ask them to come over to the house right away."

He led Dove into the cabin and poured her a glass of brandy. She accepted it gratefully. After taking a deep swallow, she said, "I shouldn't have screamed like that. I probably scared the children half to death."

"No you didn't. They thought it was part of the ride."

The gravity of the situation overwhelmed him and he sat in silence, holding her hand until the back door opened and Officers MacGowan and Frazier appeared. His glance swept over the two men in the doorway, dressed as Batman and Spiderman, like two real-life heroes come to save the day. It would have seemed comical, had the situation not been so dire.

"Mick said you needed us," MacGowan said. "What's going on?"

Starting at the beginning, Dusty told them about the Sarah Waterman trial, the letters, and finally about the mannequin.

"We should head out there, have a look around," Mack Frazier said. "Don't worry, Ms. Denning. We'll find him."

MacGowan removed his Batman mask and wiped a sheen of sweat from his forehead. "He can't have gone far. I'm sure he hung around to see your reaction. That's part of the thrill for creeps like him. Let me grab my revolver out of the car and we'll go have a look around."

"I'm right behind you," Frazier said.

"Are you going to wear that mask?"

"Have to. The costume is all one piece"

"Terrific."

Visibly calmer, Dove stood. "I have to call Mark."

The words pierced Dusty through because he knew what the outcome of the phone call would be. Mark Denning would come to Shadow Lake on the fastest thing moving. He'd look at all the evidence, evaluate it, carefully and methodically. And then he'd take Dove away.

"Listen, Dove … "

"Hey Dusty?" Mick burst into the room. "Jack and Wes Mayor just showed up."

"Damn. What are they doing?"

"They're just being kind of loud, right now. I'm pretty sure they're drunk. I told them to leave, but they won't."

He cursed under his breath. He was in no mood for the village idiots and their shenanigans. Not today.

"Want me to handle it?" MacGowan asked.

Across the room, Dove stood at the window, talking softly into her cell phone. The sight brought him a ferocious stab of pain. "Just stay with her. I'll be right back."

The door slammed behind him as he strode across the lot to the rec hall, the sound of another door closing on another chapter of his life before it even began. Before the sun rose on another day, Dove's ex-husband would come.

•

"Okay, that's it. I'm leaving here right now," Mark said. "Stay put. I don't want you left alone, not even for a minute."

"Dusty thinks I should stay at Shadow Lake. He thinks the city will give this creep more places to hide, more opportunities to strike." She started to shiver uncontrollably.

"You're coming home, Dove. You can stay with Erin and me until we nail this ass."

Disconnecting the call, she returned to the living room, where MacGowan was sprawled in the recliner. "Don't look so scared, Doll. We'll shake him out. Frazier went to have a look around. The guy probably left us a clue. They usually do."

"Have you dealt with many cases like this?"

"Stalkers? Oh, yeah. Even a small town has its crazies. Sooner or later he'll trip himself up."

She poured another glass of brandy and took a sip. Desperate for something to take her mind off her fear, she steered the subject to a safer topic. "I saw your daughter at the party earlier. She's adorable."

"Yes, she is."

"How old is she?"

"Six, going on sixteen."

She settled back on the couch to listen as he related stories about his wife and daughter. Just as she allowed herself to relax, the lights went dim and the sound of shouting filled the night air. MacGowan moved to the window and peered out. "Looks like the rec hall just lost power."

A knot of fear tightened in her stomach and she hurried to the window to peer over his shoulder. The building, which moments before had been alive with twinkling lights and music, was dark and still. "I wonder what happened."

"Must have popped a breaker. It's an old building. I see Frazier coming across the lot. I'm going to go over and see what's going on."

She followed him to the door. Stalking across the lot, he called to his partner, "Hey, Frazier, I'm going to go over and see what happened. Stay with Ms. Denning, will you?"

Giving him a thumbs-up, the other man strode toward the house. As the door closed behind him, she anxiously searched the eyes behind the mask. "Did you see anything?"

He shook his head, his mouth a grim line.

Moving back to the window, she gazed across the lot. She could see shapes moving in the darkness of the building, the glow-in-the-dark scarecrows, now menacing with their eerie grins. A wave of fear shook her again and she wished for Dusty's strong, calming presence. She was peering into the darkness, hoping for a glimpse of him, when she felt a sharp, searing pain her arm. Whirling from the window, she saw that Frazier had stuck her with a hypodermic needle. "What do you think you're doing?" she cried.

She stared into the cold eyes behind the mask, the maniacally grinning mouth, already growing blurry. Her head began to spin, and she reached out, clawing the air for something to hold onto. The cold, cold eyes that watched her fall grew fuzzier still, until finally they faded away completely.

•

Dusty couldn't remember when he'd ever felt more frustrated. It had taken some doing to get the Mayor brothers to leave peacefully, but he'd managed to pull it off. He'd no sooner sent them on their way than the Dee Jay's sound system had gone down in flames. He'd lost precious minutes in helping the old fool Mickey mouse his amp well enough to limp through the evening. And all the while, his every thought was for getting back to the house. Back to Dove. He was halfway across the lot, almost home free when the entire building went dark.

"Damn it, what now?" He did an about-face and strode back to the rec hall.

"That you, Dusty?"

He turned to see McGowan's costume glowing silver in the dark as he hurried to catch up. "What's going on?"

"The damned fool probably popped a breaker with his blasted fog machine."

He walked around to the back of the building where the breaker box was located, MacGowan following close at his heels. Jerking open the door, he went numb. All of the breakers had been switched to the off position.

"That's strange," MacGowan murmured. "Who would have done that?"

"I don't know," he said, dread settling over him like a cloud. "Where's Dove?"

"She's in the house with Frazier. She's perfectly safe."

Flipping the breakers back on, he hurried to the cabin. Flinging open the door, he called her name. The living room was deserted, the vacant space where he'd last seen her mocking him with its emptiness. Panicked, he raced through the house, searching for her, while MacGowan put in a call to the police station.

Rushing back to the rec hall, Dusty signaled wildly to Mick, who was dancing with a half-naked girl in pink Playboy bunny ears. Tearing himself from her grasp, he ambled over.

"What's up?"

"Mick, I need you to keep an eye on things here."

"Why? What's going on?"

"Dove is missing. We need to get out there and look for her."

"I'm coming with you."

"No. I need you to stay at the party," he said firmly.

"To hell with the party! You might need some help out there."

"MacGowan's going with me. What I need is for you to step up to the plate and keep things under control here. Can you do that for me, please?"

Mick's anxious glance shot to the door, where MacGowan was squeezing through the crowd, and then back to Dusty's face.

"All right," he said grudgingly.

"Thank you."

"I put in a call to dispatch," MacGowan told him. "They're sending a couple of men out."

"I think we should head back to that field."

"Try to keep calm, Dusty. I don't know what happened, but Frazier's a good cop. He'll take care of her."

"Let's go."

Following the torch-lit path, they moved quickly through the woods, their ears alert to every sound. When they reached the field, MacGowan laid a restraining hand on his arm. "We don't want to walk out in the open," he whispered. Motioning for Dusty to follow, he skirted the edge of the field, picking his way through the dense bramble. Dusty's heart began to pound as they neared the maple tree. A body lay beneath it, its white skin glowing in the moonlight.

MacGowan reached it first. Turning it face-up, he cursed. Creeping up behind him, Dusty looked into the lifeless face. A wave of bile rushed up his throat and he choked it back. Mack Frazier laid on the ground, naked except his underwear, a knife protruding from his chest. For the second time in his life, Dusty experienced sheer terror as every trace of the hope he'd clung to faded into the night. Because whoever had taken Dove wasn't playing around.

He was dead serious.

Chapter Fifteen

Through the dissipating fog inside her head, Dove became aware of movement beneath her. Under the cold, hard slab on which she lay, she detected a distinct rising and falling motion, as if she were gliding on air. Or through water. Her second cognizant thought was that she was cold, so very cold. Trying to cover herself, her hands strained against the unyielding steel of hand cuffs and a third realization struck.

She was in very deep trouble.

Shifting her body to try and ease the painful cramping in her legs, she discovered that her feet were also bound. A thick band of duct tape covered her mouth. The only things accessible to her were her eyes, and she opened them quickly. Shooting glances right and left, she saw the endless sky above her. She felt rather than saw the water that surrounded her, carrying her to God knew where.

The lake air was frigid, the clouds above her, heavy with coming snow. Peering into the darkness, she saw the silhouette of a man. His long, unkempt hair fluttered in the wind and his shoulders rippled beneath the fabric of his jacket as he steadfastly worked a pair of oars. She processed the information, a sick feeling of despair seeping into her soul. He wasn't a large man, but certainly bigger than her. Certainly big enough to dump her over the side of the rowboat if he chose, no matter how much she struggled.

Despair gave way to panic and tears sprang into to her eyes. She tried to stay calm, to center herself and think through her options. Knowing she had none, that she was utterly helpless, brought anger. As the boat moved steadily toward her certain destruction, her fury mingled with her fear, causing a burst of energy to radiate from her. With every ounce of passion she owned, she hurled a silent prayer into the universe.

Help me!

Silence answered silence, and tears spilled from her eyes and down her face. Quieting herself, she reached deep inside, to her inner garden of peace. It was a place she'd discovered early on, had cultivated to help her cope with the madness of living with Sophia. Utilizing it now, she thought back to long, lazy summers spent at her Grandmother's house in Upper Darby, thought of the people she'd loved, the people who had loved her. Lastly, achingly, she thought of Dusty.

She'd lived a productive life, had been a lover, a teacher, an advocate for those who could not speak for themselves. She thought about the days and the hours and the moments that added up to her existence and took a small measure of comfort in knowing that hers had been a life worth living.

After several moments of meditation, she felt an outside energy force begin to respond. Her hands tingled as a cloud of vapor appeared beside the boat. She closed her eyes, and when she opened them again, Chelsea was watching her intently. In a moment of supreme clarity, she understood why, since her arrival at Shadow Lake, she had experienced a hyper-sensitivity to the spirit world. Why she'd seen the dead more clearly than ever before, indeed, had at times been unable to distinguish them from the living. Because her own death was imminent. The realization brought fresh tears and she gazed deeply into Chelsea's eyes.

Please. Help me.

Chelsea's eyes were luminous as they looked on her, glowing with compassion. In a fraction of an instant Chelsea was hovering beside the man, her face inches from his, her compassion changed to dark, burning anger. As if feeling her icy breath, the man shivered and turned up the collar of his jacket. Dove watched in morbid fascination as Chelsea reached out her hand and struck his face.

Turning sharply, he fixed his angry gaze on Dove. She gasped beneath the duct tape, trying to make sense of the face that registered in her brain.

"Don't start your voo doo crap with me, you hear?"

Turning back to his work, he pulled harder on the oars, propelling the boat swiftly toward its destination. They rode the waves in silence, the three of them. Dove. Chelsea. And Reverend

Wesley Wallace.

Time lost all meaning. What could have been moments or hours later, she felt the thud of earth beneath her. The pastor got out and heaved the rowboat onto shore. Grabbing her roughly, he lifted her out and dumped her onto the ground, then pushed the boat back into the lake, setting it adrift on the waves. It was Dusty's boat, she saw, the one he took out every morning to watch the sunrise. Tears came again. She'd hoped to one day experience those quiet, solemn moments with him. And now she'd never see him again.

Returning to where she lay, the pastor pulled her from the ground, slung her over his shoulder, and carried her toward a building. Illuminated in the moonlight, she saw the sign above the door: *Jerry's Bait and Tackle Shop*, and she shuddered.

The building was pitch dark inside and smelled of dust and stale beer. Carrying her to a back room, he dumped her onto the floor and fumbled with an oil lamp. As the room flickered to life, she saw a sleeping bag rolled out on the floor, surrounded by empty beer and tuna fish cans, and she understood the fear she'd felt when she first encountered the building. This was where evil lived. This was where her captor had been hiding out, stalking her, waiting for this moment.

He set about tearing a stack of old newspapers into shreds. Balling them into tight wads, he packed them around her. And then as if finally satisfied with the nest he'd built, he spoke. "You ruined my life and my reputation, and now you shall receive just recompense for your actions."

She stared at him, uncomprehending.

"Speak in your defense!" Leaning over her, he grabbed a corner of the tape and ripped it from her mouth. The pain was ferocious, but she would not flinch, would not die cowering at this maniac's feet. She drew a breath, knowing her words would either save or damn her.

"You're mistaken."

He spoke again, as if she hadn't said a word. "I was a good and faithful servant of the cross. I had position, power. I was someone! And then you showed up." He glared at her, his eyes glittering with madness. "From the day I set eyes on you, it all went wrong. In trying to rid the town of evil, I became a laughingstock to my flock. But that was your intention all along, wasn't it?"

"I ... I don't ..."

"Wasn't it?" He took her by the shoulders and shook her violently. Her teeth banged together and a lightning flash of pain shot through her neck.

"Afterwards I couldn't move on because thanks to you no other church would have me. You left me with no home, no money. No self respect. I fasted and I prayed for deliverance, and in a vision it was revealed to me. It all became clear." He began to pace. In the flickering lamp light she saw that his aura was the dirty gray of illness and evil intent. She stared at him in horror, knowing his tirade was the ranting of a lunatic.

He turned to face her again. "That night at the old hotel, when I saw you practicing your witchcraft ... I rebuked you, and what did you do?" he thundered. "You cast a spell on me, a curse that brought me to ruination." Crossing the room, he opened a cupboard and retrieved a pile of rags and a can of gasoline.

"And so I went after you. I followed you to Philadelphia, intending to plead with you for mercy, to see if I could implore you, out of human decency, to remove the curse. And when I got there, what did I discover? I discovered you ... ruining another man's life. Persecuting the church. Evil, evil sorceress."

"I was not persecuting the church. That man killed a child."

"He annihilated a force of evil, a witch! Just as I'm going to tonight."

She became aware of pure fury swirling in the air, coupled with all of the energy and frustration of adolescence, and she knew that Chelsea was once again present. Without warning, a can of pork 'n beans flew across the room and struck his face, leaving an angry red welt.

He stared at her for a moment in disbelief, and then, in a fit of anger, yanked her up by the hair and leveled his fist at her nose. She heard the sickening crunch of bone on bone, felt a shock of pain, and then the warm rush of blood filling her mouth.

The display of violence seemed to whip Chelsea into a frenzy. A tool box flew across the room, crashing against the wall behind the pastor's head, a jumble of fishing lures and bobbers spilling out onto the floor. Following the tool box, an assortment of rusted tools were pulled from a rack on the wall and flung in his direction, and then a fisherman's creel with a broken hasp.

"Reprobate!" He thundered. "Sinner!"

A shower of fish hooks cascaded from above him, their pointed ends sticking into his clothes and hair. Enraged, he began to kick her. With no way to shield herself from the blows, she lay helpless at his feet, writhing in agony as his foot crashed into her legs, her spine, her rib cage. She couldn't breathe, couldn't speak. All she could do was send out a desperate plea.

Chelsea! Stop!

Abruptly, the room fell silent. The pastor stood above her, panting with exertion. "Lord Almighty, God of justice, receive this sin offering from the hands of thy humble servant."

He grabbed up the gas can, twisted off the cap, and showered her with gasoline.

Dove watched in terror as, his lips twisted into a cruel smile, he pulled a packet of wooden matches from his pocket.

Chapter Sixteen

Dusty stood at the water's edge, staring across the lake with unseeing eyes as he tried to stave off the hysteria that gnawed at his guts. Falling apart wouldn't help anything. His body cried out for alcohol, but his rational mind knew that drinking wouldn't really help, either. The only thing that would calm the tempest raging inside him was to have Dove back in his arms, safe and unharmed.

He clutched her scarf, only vaguely aware of the frenzied activity taking place around him. Within minutes of MacGowan's call to the police station, reporting a slain officer, the campground had been swarming with cops. They'd questioned everyone at the party. No one saw anything out of the ordinary. Not surprising, he thought, considering the building had been plunged into total darkness. Whoever had taken Dove had fine-tuned his plan to perfection.

Some of the detectives had set up a headquarters in the house, their maps and equipment spread across the kitchen table, every town within a fifty-mile radius of Shadow Lake circled in red. Others were out combing the woods, searching for Dove with no results. It was ten o'clock. Close to two hours since her disappearance and Dusty knew with a sick certainty they were running out of time. Helplessness rendered him inert, and he felt again the excruciating pain of having let something beautiful slip from his grasp, felt the absolute, gut twisting guilt of knowing he was to blame. He'd let her down. He would have given anything to be able to turn back time, to have stayed by her side. To make good on his promise to protect her. If only they could find her in time. If only she could be safely returned to him, he'd never let her go again. If only …

He gazed out at the lake, as if in its quiet depths he might find the answers he sought. "Oh, Dove. Honey, where are you?"

In answer he heard only the barking of dogs. Their cries rose up in the night, mirroring the agonized howling in his soul. When the K-9 unit arrived, Dusty had been assigned the task of finding one of her garments in the hope the dogs could track her scent. Going through her things was torture. He'd handed over her jacket, keeping a scarf for himself. Now he stood in the dark, clinging to it like a lifeline.

The sheer irony of the situation was not lost on him. Thinking about it, he felt a bitter twinge of resentment. She'd eased the way for so many others, had been blessed with the ability to see both past and future. And yet she hadn't been able to foresee her own misfortune … Or had she?

His mind began to race as, like lightning from out of the sky, a chilling thought struck him. And suddenly, he knew where she was.

•

The flame danced in the pastor's hand. Hungry, it hovered, flaring up, reaching out for oxygen, for something to sustain its life. Mere feet away, gasoline seeped through the fabric of Dove's dress, beckoning to the fire.

It would come within seconds; the initial shock of her body igniting. The stench would be unbelievable as it devoured her skin. The rest of the process would be agonizingly slow as fire licked at her tissues and organs. She supposed the pain would be ferocious.

A sheen of sweat broke out on her face. *Just do it*, she thought. *Just do it and get it the hell over with …* But no, there had to be a way. If she could stay alive for just a moment longer, the universe would intervene. It would show her the way to save herself. It had to.

She watched, mesmerized by the pastor's every movement. He let the flame burn down to his fingertips, and then finally, blew it out. He stared at her for a long, bloodcurdling moment. And then he smiled. "I'm not a cruel man, Ms. Denning. But desperate times call for desperate measures. Now that you understand the enormity of the situation, I'm sure the two of us can reach some sort of compromise."

Terror wedged like a thick knot in her throat. She choked it back. "What sort of compromise?"

"I'd like you to remove the curse."

"And then you'll let me go?"

He smiled again. "And then I'll let you go."

It was a bald faced lie, it couldn't be anything else. The fact that he had Frazier's costume, along with his handcuffs, told her he'd already committed one crime that night.

One more wouldn't make a difference. Still, this new card he'd thrown onto the table would buy her precious time. She'd have to be very careful how she played it.

"I don't believe you."

His smile widened. "Madame, you don't have a choice."

"Untie me. Show me you're a man of your word."

"You're awfully demanding for someone in your position."

"And you're awfully smug for someone in yours."

His smile wavered. "Meaning?"

A muffled thud came from the front of the building, as if something heavy had been thrown at the window. Wallace's expression darkened. "I warn you, this had better not be more of your shenanigans."

He pulled a gun from the waistband of his pants. Its sleek barrel glinted in the lamp light, and Dove's breath caught. She'd lived with a cop long enough to know that she was looking at a patrolman's service revolver. Frazier was dead, then. There was no hope for her.

Holding the gun out in front of him, Wallace crept from the room. She could hear the soft thump of his footsteps as he moved around in the room next door, could feel the nervous energy he left behind. Moments later he returned. "It must have been a bird. They're always flying into the windows. At least I hope for your sake that's all it was."

He pulled a hankie from his pocket and mopped his sweating brow. "I certainly hope your boyfriend won't be foolish enough to try and be a hero or he'll end up at the bottom of the lake, like his daughter."

"And how do you know about that?"

"This is a small town. A small town with a lot of big mouths." He grinned cruelly. "Once you get them started, these people just won't shut up. Mr. Martin's good friends couldn't wait to tell a perfect stranger about the homeless drunk. About how his daughter got knocked up and jumped out of a boat rather than face him. Some father, eh?"

Dove could feel the room vibrating with sudden energy. The oil lamp flickered as Chelsea moved past it and hovered beside the pastor. *That's not true!* she shrieked.

Ignorant of the tempest he'd created, he dropped to a squat in front of Dove. "Now where were we?"

"You were going to undo my hands and feet."

"I've told you, you're in no—"

He was inches away. So close she could smell his sweat and the alcohol on his breath. Seizing the moment, she drew up both of her legs. With every ounce of force she owned, she struck out with her feet, catching him beneath the chin. He fell backward with a tremendous crash.

Moving quickly, Dove rolled onto her side. Pain shot through her rib cage, stealing her breath away. Ignoring it, she struggled to her knees. Trying to stand, she lost her balance, fell to the floor, and began the slow process again. She heard a scuffling behind her and then felt a searing pain as Wallace's foot connected with her back. She tumbled face first onto the floor and lay there, inert, knowing she'd squandered her only chance.

"That was a very foolish move, Ms. Denning." His voice was devoid of emotion, terrifying in its emptiness. "A very foolish move."

There was a moment of silence, and then she heard a soft scraping sound and the unmistakable sizzle of a match flaring to life. The room began to spin. A blessed numbness spread through her body and she knew she was going into shock. Grateful for its anesthetizing effect, she pressed her cheek into the floor, closed her eyes, and let his voice fade away.

"This time there will be no mercy."

"You're damned right about that."

In a moment of confusion the entire scenario changed. Dove opened her eyes, watching in bewilderment as Dusty burst into the room, tackling Wallace from behind. At the sight of him, Chelsea let loose a piercing wail. The sickening sound of fists connecting with bone filled the room as the two men fought.

The situation shifted again as Wallace retrieved the revolver from his waistband. Dove screamed as he fired wildly into the air, bullets ricocheting off the walls and ceiling. She struggled to maintain consciousness as the room erupted into a mêlée of broken glass and flying objects. Chelsea hurled herself at the windows and then at the walls, all the while wailing disconsolately. With a strength born of fury, she hurled an old, chipped coffee mug in Wallace's direction, neatly clipping his ear. With a howl of pain, he dropped the gun and sent it clattering to the floor. Dove heard a wooden pallet splinter as the two men resumed their grappling. She heard Dusty groan as Wallace landed a punch, saw the blood seep from his skin as Wallace drew a fish hook down his face. Chelsea howled with rage as she sent a tarnished pocket watch sailing through the air. It struck Wallace in the forehead with a sickening crack and sent him toppling backward. Grabbing the gun, Dusty stood to his feet. Sweating, panting, he aimed it at Wallace.

The banging of the door was like thunder in the sudden silence of the room. "Don't do it, Dusty."

Dove turned toward the voice. Through a haze of pain, it registered that Officer MacGowan was in the room. He stood just inside the doorway, his revolver drawn.

"Give me one good reason not to, Joe." Dusty raised his free arm and wiped the sweat from his eyes. "Just one."

"I'll give you two. First one would be that little gal over there." With a nod of his head he indicated Dove. "You don't want her to watch you gun a man down in cold blood."

As Dusty fixed his gaze on Dove, tears filled his eyes. "He needs to pay for what he's done. A lifetime behind bars wouldn't be enough. I won't take a chance on some courtroom circus."

"Which brings me to my second reason, which would be personal." Crossing the room, MacGowan pointed his revolver at Wallace's chest. "There won't be any court rooms. Frazier was my partner for more than ten years. He was like a brother. We had an agreement about cop killers. A mutual promise." He clicked the safety off. "This is my score to settle, Dusty. Not yours."

Wallace's eyes bulged. "You can't be serious. You're a lawman. You can't just shoot an unarmed man in cold blood. I deserve a trial, a jury of my peers. I deserve—"

A thunderous blast shook the room, and then Dove saw Wallace fall to the floor for the last time, a dark pool of blood spreading across his chest.

In the echo of the thunder, MacGowan spoke. "I'm going out to the car. I'm going to radio in that shots were fired in self defense. And then I'm going to call an ambulance for the lady." He removed a set of keys from his pocket and threw them to Dusty on his way out.

Pulling out his pocket knife, Dusty sliced through the fishing rope that bound her feet. When he'd unlocked the hand cuffs, he gently pulled her into his arms. Tears spilled from his eyes. "I never thought I'd see you again. Oh, God. Are you all right?"

"I will be," she said through parched lips. "As soon as you hold me."

He stroked her hair. "I'm sorry, Dove. I'm so sorry."

Moments later MacGowan returned. "I saw you take off like a bat out of hell," he told Dusty. "Figured you must know something I didn't, so I followed you. I should have radioed then for backup, but I didn't want an audience. I'm guessing you felt the same way. I'm glad as hell it worked out like it did."

His voice trailed away in silence. Neither of them answered. Neither were listening. Dove's head was spinning. Every bone and muscle in her body ached. Resting her cheek against Dusty's chest, she took comfort in the sound of his heartbeat, and the reassuring wail of sirens in the distance.

Chapter Seventeen

Three days later Dove lay on Emma's sofa, nestled into a cocoon of soft blankets and fluffy white pillows. Wendy knelt at her feet, applying a second coat of electric blue polish to her toenails.

"Are you sure it's my color?" Dove asked skeptically.

"Of course it's your color. It's totally fab on you."

Returning from the kitchen, Emma set a bowl of popcorn on the coffee table in front of her. "Are you warm enough, Dove? Would you like another blanket?"

"I'm fine, Emma. Please don't feel you have to fuss over me."

"I like to fuss over you. You're my f-friend." She grabbed a handful of popcorn. "We've got time for one more movie before the guys get back. Which one should we watch?"

"Failure to Launch!" Wendy cried.

"We already watched that one y-yesterday."

"I know, but Matthew McConaughey is so hot."

Dove smiled. In the short time she'd been home from the hospital Emma and Wendy had appointed themselves her personal caretakers. Emma's sweet spirit was a balm to her battered nerves and Wendy was starting to feel like a daughter. Simply put, she felt loved. It wasn't a bad feeling at all.

The incident on Halloween had left her with a concussion and some bruised ribs and a collection of contusions in varying shades of purple and gold covered her face and body. But she was alive. Blessedly, wonderfully alive.

"Let's go with *Steel Magnolias*," Emma said, retrieving the DVD from the top of the pile. "It's always been one of my favorites."

"Oh, all right," Wendy conceded grudgingly.

Though the movie was also one of her favorites, Dove had a hard time concentrating on it. Her mind was filled to overflowing with all that had happened during her short stay at Shadow Lake. She thought of Wallace, with his grizzly scheme to exact revenge for a crime she hadn't committed, and of his own gruesome end. She thought of Chelsea, and how she'd intervened. Then she thought of Dusty and a familiar surge of warmth spread through her. She'd cared for him before, but what he'd done for her that night had elevated her feelings to an entirely different level. He'd saved her life, and at the same time, had stolen her heart.

And she hadn't even had a chance to thank him.

He'd been scarce since her return from the hospital. He'd moved into the guest cottage the day Dove was released from the hospital so she could stay in the guest room, under Emma's watchful eye. She'd barely seen him, let alone had a chance to speak with him privately. *So much to talk about,* she thought with a sigh, *and so little time.*

Later that afternoon, as the final movie credits flashed across the screen, Shane and Mick appeared in the living room.

"Is it safe to come in?" Shane asked, giving Emma a heart-stopping grin.

"Yep. Girls' Day In is n-now officially over."

He scooped Emma up in his arms and nuzzled her. "Good, cause we're officially starving."

"What sounds good for dinner?"

"I vote we go to Chubbys for pizza and wings," Mick piped up.

"Ooh, that sounds good," Wendy said. "Can I go, too?"

"You'd better call your aunt Polly and make sure it's all right," Mick cautioned. "Remember what happened last time."

A frown creased Emma's brow. "D-do you feel up to it, Dove?"

Though it had been a peaceful, lovely day, Dove felt fatigue setting in. "Actually, Em, I think I'd rather stay here. That last bowl of popcorn did me in."

"I hate to leave you here alone," Emma hedged.

"Don't be silly. I'll be perfectly all right."

"I'll be around, Emma." Hearing Dusty's voice behind her, Dove turned. Their eyes met, and she saw in his a quiet longing that mirrored her own.

"Good, then it's all settled," Shane said. "Last one in the truck gets to buy the pizza."

Shouting and laughing, the teens raced from the room with Emma and Shane following. When the front door closed behind them, Dusty sat down in the chair across from her. "How are you, Dove?"

She smiled. "Better than I look, probably."

"You look beautiful." His eyes met hers briefly before falling away and Dove could only wonder at the reason for his sudden shyness with her.

"I never got a chance to thank you for what you did for me that night," she said. "You saved my life. Thank you doesn't seem nearly enough to say."

"Thank me? I was afraid you'd never want to see me again."

"Why on earth would you think that?"

"I screwed up, Dove. You trusted me and I put you in jeopardy."

"Please don't blame yourself. I don't. Not for any of it."

"There were so many things I should have done differently." He raked his fingers through his hair. "I saw Wallace on the trails the weekend you arrived here. If I'd paid more attention he wouldn't have been able to get so close. And if I hadn't left you and gone to the rec hall that night none of it would have happened. I'm so sorry you had to go through that."

"It's over now. We have to put it in the past. We have to move on." Together, she thought, but didn't say.

He sighed. "That's not an easy thing to do. I close my eyes at night and the whole ugly scenario plays out in my mind. The most disturbing part is that if MacGowan hadn't shot him, I believe I would have. He was an evil human being." An involuntary shudder rippled through him. "You must have been terrified, those hours you were alone with him."

She pulled in a breath and slowly released it, not at all certain he was ready for the truth. "Dusty," she said softly. "I wasn't completely alone. Chelsea was there with me the entire time."

His eyes sought hers, and in them, she could see how deeply her words had cut him. "She was?"

"Uh-huh."

"That would explain a lot," he said softly.

"Would you like to talk about it?"

He was silent for a moment, clearly struggling. Then he stood.

"Maybe some time, but not right now." He came to her and gently kissed her cheek. "Get some rest."

She'd known the words would be hard to hear, but a part of her had hoped the revelation would bring them together. Instead he was running away, leaving her, both physically and emotionally, and all she could do was watch him go.

•

Dusty's rowboat had been recovered within a few hours of Dove's return. It had washed up on the shore at the campground as if it, too, had missed the sunrise mornings. Early the next day, Dusty paddled out into the lake, Dove's words from the night before still echoing inside his head. The landscape was as cold and uninviting as the frigid temperature, the trees that lined the shore stripped of their foliage and thin patches of ice coating the water's surface. The chill November air stung his face and made his eyes water. Later that day or maybe the next he'd put the rowboat away for the winter. As it was, he needed one more sunrise morning on the lake.

He'd laid awake for most of the night thinking about the things she told him, trying to fathom that Chelsea's spirit had appeared to her that night. How often in the last three days had his thoughts wandered back to the tackle shop and the incredible images that registered in his brain while he fought with Wesley Wallace? Items hurling through the air, seemingly of their own accord, and more disturbing, the long shadow that seemed to fall across him when he entered the building, leaving him bitterly cold, while at the same time, feverish with emotion. It wasn't until much later that he recalled how vividly he'd smelled the sweet scent of Chelsea's perfume.

Yes, his daughter had been there. Of that he had no doubt.

Dove once told him she suspected Chelsea was waiting for his permission to leave. Pondering that throughout the long, lonely night, he remembered lying face-down in the sand the night they pulled her body from the lake, and how he'd begged her not to go. A bitter sob stuck in his throat with the realization that honoring that request had kept his precious child in torment these eight long years.

Reaching his favorite inlet, he let the oars slide to his lap. If Chelsea would appear to Dove, a perfect stranger, then surely she'd appear to him. Closing his eyes, he concentrated on filling his lungs with air, his mind with calming thoughts. After a long moment of meditation, he spoke.

"I remember when you were little and I used to make you hold my hand in a crowded parking lot, or whenever we crossed a busy street," he said. "I needed to keep you close by, to know that you were safe. As you grew up, I couldn't stop thinking of you as that little girl I had to watch over and protect." Tears stung his eyes and he blinked them back. "I know I smothered you, Chelsea. I know I made you feel like I didn't trust you. But it wasn't that. It was that great big, wide world out there I didn't trust. I thought of all the things that could happen, and I couldn't bear the thought of a life without you. I still can't."

His voice cracked and he pulled in a breath. "But I need for you to leave me now. I need to know that you're in a place of rest, and peace. That you're safe. So if you can hear me, I want you to know that I love you very much, Chelsea. And that's why I'm asking you to leave here now. Do it for me, honey. And do it for you." He waited in the quiet for some sort of sign that she'd heard. When none came, he bowed his head in sadness. He'd done it wrong again.

He knew the reason was probably the negative aura surrounding him, the sorrow he couldn't quite seem to shake off. Sorrow born of the pain of losing something else he loved. Dove. Emma had said she was leaving at the end of the week. He'd so hoped…

Hoped for what? That she'd want to stay on permanently at Shadow Lake, give up her life in the city, her career, for him? It was a nice fantasy, but Dusty Martin didn't live in a make-believe world. Not anymore. Seeing Mark Denning at Dove's bedside in the hospital had woken him up to reality. Dove's ex-husband was everything Dusty wasn't; polished, well educated, good looking. He hadn't been able to hold her. What possible chance could Dusty have?

Pulling back on the oars, he turned the boat toward home. She still felt something for him. He'd seen it the moment their eyes met last night, the same as he'd seen the hurting when he'd left her so abruptly. God. He'd have done anything to avoid putting that look in her eyes.

But it was best this way. Better to have her leave Shadow Lake still loving him, than stay and grow to despise him. He'd send her away for the same reason he'd tried to send his beloved Chelsea away. For her own good.

Falling in love with Dove had been easy, had happened almost overnight. Falling out of love with her would be a slow, agonizing process. But he'd get through it somehow. He'd get over her the same way he'd conquered his addiction to alcohol. One day, one moment, one craving at a time.

Chapter Eighteen

On Friday afternoon Dove made her way up the path, her heart heavy with sadness. Dusty had been strangely cool when they'd spoken last, on Tuesday evening. She'd attributed that to the twofold strain of Halloween night, and her revelation that Chelsea had been with her at the bait and tackle shop. She'd thought with time he'd come around. But it was clear he wasn't coming around. If anything he was moving farther away.

She'd been trying to get alone with him all week with no luck. Today she'd walked down the path with a spring of excitement in her step. Yesterday morning she'd called in a favor with Kelly Borchardt, a long-time friend who also happened to be the Head of Personnel at the university. When Dove explained her situation, Kelly agreed to give Dusty a position in the Operations and Maintenance department. The pay and benefits were good and the job seemed like a perfect fit. She was anxious to run it past him and see if the idea held any appeal. Though she felt certain he was home, he hadn't come to the door. He was definitely giving her the brush-off treatment, and it hurt like hell. Trudging back up the path, she brushed away a tear. Had their love affair meant so little to him?

When she returned to the cabin, Emma was setting the table for lunch. She glanced up in surprise when Dove re-entered the house. "I thought you were going to invite Dusty out for lunch."

"Evidently he isn't interested."

Retrieving a set of soup bowls from the cupboard, she gave Dove a sidelong glance. "I know it's none of my business, but if you want to t-tell me about it, you can."

"We spent some time together while you were gone and got

to know each other pretty well. I've come to care for him, Emma. More than I thought possible."

"Does he know that?"

"I thought it was obvious." She shrugged, managed a smile. "Guess I was wrong."

"Then you should tell him."

"There's no point in it. My life is in Philly. Dusty's is here. He's not interested in relocating. He's already made that clear."

"There's got to be room for some kind of compromise. He cares for you, Dove, I know he does. I've never seen him like this before. To t-tell you the truth, Shane and I have been worried about him. He's miserable." She added softly, "That's what happens when you try and run away from love."

Later that afternoon Dove took a last drive around the lake to say goodbye to Polly and Wendy. Over a dinner of Polly's homemade chicken pot pie she learned about the migrating habits of blue birds, and the local campaign Polly had launched to attract the elusive songbirds back to New York State. She was a fascinating woman and Dove was sorry she hadn't had the opportunity to get to know her better.

As Dove was leaving, Wendy followed her to the car and threw her arms around her in an impulsive hug. "I'm gonna miss you so much."

"I meant what I said about you coming to visit me in Philly over Christmas break, Wendy. In the meantime you've got my number if you ever want to talk."

"Thanks Ms. Denning," she whispered. "For being my friend."

Dove gave her a squeeze. "I might say the same to you."

Pulling away, Wendy smiled. "Peace out."

Returning to the cabin, Dove tried to interest herself in a TV program Shane and Emma were watching, but her recalcitrant thoughts kept returning to Dusty. After an hour she gave up on the program, knowing she wouldn't be able to think about anything else until she'd set things straight. Gathering her resolve, she turned her footsteps back toward his cottage. She was leaving for Philadelphia early in the morning. Dusty was obviously not interested in hearing all that was in her heart, but at the very least, she was going to say goodbye.

Walking resolutely to the door, she raised her fist and knocked.

The sound reverberated in the air, echoing the pounding of her heart. She was scared, so very scared of what he might say to her. But even more unsettling was the thought of leaving here with things unresolved between them.

Hearing no movement inside, she peered in the window. The soft glow of a table lamp illuminated the cottage and she saw the blinds on the sliding door across the room were open, a dark figure silhouetted on the deck out back. Gathering her coat around her, she stepped from the porch.

She was halfway across the yard when a violent stinging sensation started in her hands. An icy blast of air slapped her face, stealing her breath away. Bracing herself, she closed her eyes and took several deep breaths. When she opened them again Chelsea stood before her.

What do you want, Chelsea?

He's crying.

I'm sorry.

It's because of me, I know it is.

I'm very sorry.

I need your help.

She hesitated, knowing the conversation could lead to only one place. *What do you want me to do?*

I want to talk to him, to tell him how it was. I can't do that without you. Please? Will you help me?

Fingers of fear curled around her heart. Was she strong enough to do what Chelsea wanted? An emotional house of cards, the weight of just one more might very well cause her mental collapse. But looking into Chelsea's wide, pleading eyes, she knew she had no choice except to do as she asked.

Alright.

Closing her eyes again, she became aware of the crackle of electricity in the air and a low, almost imperceptible whining sound. Static electricity prickled her skin and caused her hands to tremble. The whining grew louder as images of Chelsea filled her brain. They flashed across her mind, faster and faster until the images blurred together and all that was left was the essence of Chelsea's spirit.

She felt herself swirling, spinning, as if she'd fallen headlong into a tunnel, her stomach turning inside out until she feared she'd be ill. Swirling and swirling as alien energy fought to gain entry into her being. This time she didn't fight it. Embracing it, she felt herself diminishing as the energy grew stronger and stronger, until at last it consumed her completely.

•

Dusty stood on the back deck, warily scanning the empty scrap of beach front. A moment before, he thought he'd seen something hovering above the lake. But now, scrutinizing the horizon, he realized it was just his imagination playing tricks on him.

A light snow sifted down from the sky, tickling his face and arms. He embraced the cold, savored the sensation of feeling. He'd been numb for the last three days, since he'd learned of Dove's plan to return to Philly first thing Saturday morning. Turning his face to the snow, he spoke the words aloud. "At this time tomorrow, she'll be gone."

The words slammed into his heart like a fist. Everything inside him fought against them, but logically, he knew there was nothing he could do except let her go. Her suggestion that he go back with her had kept him awake more nights than one, but in the end the answer was clear. He had nothing to offer her. He'd be a cross, a millstone around her neck. Better to let her go, no matter how much it hurt.

Gazing out at the snow-scattered landscape, all of the hopes he'd allowed himself, all the foolish fantasies of love and companionship rose up to taunt him. He felt them slipping away, and in their place, the deep, dark emptiness of his life stretching out before him, endless, hopeless. Tears sprang to his eyes. What was the point in a life like that?

"Daddy, please don't be sad."

The words nearly stopped his heart. Turning, he saw Dove standing in the yard, gazing at him with large, vacant eyes.

"Dove?"

"It's me, Daddy. Chelsea."

It was Dove's voice, but the tone and inflections were those of his daughter. A sob caught in his throat. "Chelsea?"

She took a hesitant step toward him. "I loved holding your hand."

"What?"

"What you said earlier? You were wrong. When I was little,

holding your hand made me feel safe. Just being with you made me feel safe and loved. I know it must have seemed like I didn't listen, but I did. I heard every word you ever said to me."

A thousand words of love filled his mind and heart, but he couldn't force even one of them past the lump that thickened in his throat.

"I remember how you always used to tell me to stand up for my convictions, even if everyone in the whole world thought I was wrong. And not to be afraid of facing up to responsibility. You think I took my life that night to avoid facing you, but it wasn't like that."

Hot tears blurred his vision. "Oh, Chelsea, I never meant ..."

"I'm sorry I took the boat out without asking, but I had to meet Tyler. I had to find out where I stood. You understand that, don't you?"

Unable to speak, he nodded.

"I talked him into taking his father's boat and meeting me on the lake. I wish I'd never done that."

He gripped the railing until his knuckles burned. "What happened, honey?"

"We got in a fight when I told him about the baby. He said it was over between us and then he just drove away, like it was no big deal. I was so mad, madder than I've ever been. I took off my sandals and threw them at him. Which was stupid, because he was already driving away. Instead of hitting Tyler I accidentally knocked your flag into the water. The blue and gold one mom had made for your birthday. I leaned over the side of the boat to try and get it and ..." She choked on a sob.

A wave of nausea rose up inside him. "Oh, honey ..."

"I fell in. I didn't have a life jacket on, and the boat kept going. I swam after it as hard as I could, but I couldn't catch up. I tried so hard, Daddy. I never wanted to hurt you. I never wanted to leave you." Her voice dropped to a whisper. "I love you, daddy. So much."

The words wrenched deep, wracking sobs from his chest. He opened his arms to her and she ran to him, fell into his embrace, and wept against his neck. "I never wanted to leave you."

He held her tightly, savoring the feel of her in his arms, knowing it was for the last time. Finally, he released her. "Chelsea, listen to me. I love you more than anything in this world. More than my own life. But I want you to leave here now."

She moaned softly and tightened her grip on him.

Despite his breaking heart, he managed a sternness he'd never quite mastered in her lifetime. "What happened, happened. There's no taking it back, though I'd give anything if I could. I know there's something better out there and you have to move on to it, do you hear me? You can't stay where you are any longer. It's not good for either of us."

"But you asked me not to. You begged me. I don't understand…"

"That was a long time ago. More than eight years have passed since then. I want you to move on now. I need you to."

"I don't know how," she whispered.

The words he'd read in his book came back to him with crystal clarity, and all at once he knew what to do.

"Let go of it, Chelsea," he said softly. "Allow yourself to let go of what happened that night. Imagine that you're a bird let out of a cage, flying away, high above the world. Feel it in your heart. Let yourself see it!"

He held his breath, struggling to fill his own mind with thoughts of joy and peace, until at last he felt a gradual pulling away. Not a physical sensation, but one of something being torn from inside of him. Gradually her grip on him loosened, until her arms became slack at her sides. A humming sound seemed to vibrate in the air around him and he knew beyond a doubt it was the sound of Chelsea's leave-taking.

Suddenly, he had the sensation of being enveloped in a thick fog as images of Chelsea flashed across his brain. His emotions crashed against one another like thunder crashing on the waves. Tears poured down his face. It was agony. He was losing his baby daughter again. He couldn't bear it. Not for another moment.

Just when he was certain the sorrow of his own tears would drown him, the sensations began subside. He clung to her fiercely, shielding her as best he could against the storm. And then the tempest faded away into eerie silence, and there was only him and Dove.

Chapter Nineteen

Dove awakened to the delicious sensation of hands gliding over her skin—strong, capable hands, soothing the stress from her neck and shoulders. She took a moment to enjoy the scent of Dusty's nearness, the feel of his body close to hers. When his hands moved to her lower back, she moaned softly and opened her eyes.

Stopping his work, he gazed down at her, his expression filled with tenderness. "I was starting to get worried," he said.

"How long have I been out?"

"A couple of hours."

"How did it go?"

A small shadow moved across his face. "She's gone."

She squeezed his hand. "Are you okay?"

"I am. I really am. I feel at peace for the first time since the accident. I don't know how to thank you, Dove."

She patted the empty space beside her on the mattress. "Lay down with me."

After a moment's hesitation, he lay down beside her and gathered her into his arms. She moved into his embrace, not speaking, taking comfort in his nearness and the warmth that radiated from his eyes. Finally, he broke the silence.

"I don't want to let you go, Dove." He brushed his fingertips across his cheek. "God help me, I feel like I've found a part of me that's been missing all my life."

She gazed into his eyes, waiting for him to continue.

"I know I've only known you for a short time. Emma says the heart loves whom it loves. I believe that's true."

The confession went straight through her soul and for a moment she couldn't breathe. "Do you love me, Dusty?"

"Yes, I do."

"Then come to Philly with me."

"I wish I could. I'd give anything if things were different." His eyes dropped away. "I'm not good enough for you, Dove. I have nothing to offer a woman like you."

She gently placed her fingers over his lips. "You're kind and honest and strong. You restore my peace of mind, and make me feel complete. I want everything you are, and nothing that you're not."

"But I don't even have a job. I can't let you to support me."

"That's something I've been wanting to talk to you about." She drew a deep breath, hoping she hadn't overstepped. "I spoke with a colleague of mine at the university. There's an opening in the Operations and Maintenance department. I pulled a couple of strings. They'd like to interview you as soon as possible."

"You did that for me?"

"For us."

His eyes filled with tears and he blinked them back. "Tonight, Chelsea finally moved on. It's time for me to do the same. I don't know where to start, exactly. But I know I love you."

"I love you, too."

"Then I guess that's where we start," he whispered.

He kissed her, and it was like returning home after a lifetime of aimless wandering. She snuggled deeper into his embrace, thankful for the gift of new beginnings, eager to experience all the magic the future had to give.

• • •

M. Jean Pike

Photo by Sharon Burr

Abandoned buildings. Restless spirits. Love that lasts forever. These are a few of M. Jean Pike's favorite things. A professional writer since 1996, Ms. Pike combines a passion for romance with a keen interest in the supernatural to bring readers unforgettable stories of life, love and the inner workings of the human heart. She writes from her home on a quiet country road in upstate New York.

www.freewebs.com/mjeanpike

CPSIA information can be obtained at www.ICGtesting.com
Printed in the USA
LVOW122041220312

274405LV00001B/32/P